Monkey Casserole

Also by SpearPoint Publications

Embracing Evil
Mizeta Moon
(eBook)

Snapshots: Flash Stories from Random Lives
Howard Schneider with Mizeta Moon

Monkey Casserole: 33 Selected Short Stories
Howard Schneider, Mizeta Moon & Linda Burk
(eBook)

Word Storms: Original Fiction
Howard Schneider, Mizeta Moon & Silver Gladstar

Aliens, Fish Tales % Flying Hooves
Mizeta Moon

Survival: Collected Short Fiction
Howard Schneider and Mizeta Moon

Danger Wears Pantyhose!
Mizeta Moon

Against All Evil
Old-Time Radio-Style Serial Adventures
Howard Schneider

45 Pieces of Turkish Delight
Patricia Morgan

Through the Kaleidoscope
Short Fiction from the Mind of Mizeta Moon
Mizeta Moon

Seeds of Change
Patricia Morgan

Fortunate But Fated
Maurice Posada

Just Plain Lucky
Tom Lloyd

Monkey Casserole

33 Selected Short Stories

By

Howard Schneider
Mizeta Moon
&
Linda Burk

SpearPoint Publications

Published in the United States by SpearPoint
Publications, Portland, OR

2021

Cover created by Zap Graphics, Portland, Oregon

ISBN: 9798577512187

Contents

Monkeys in the Mango Trees

By Howard Schneider

The Problem

Early on a Sunday morning, Ajit Kapoor woke to raucous shrieking outside his one-room, mud-brick hut. It was Padma, his beloved wife of two months.

Sunday was the day Ajit slept late to catch up on much-needed rest—the only day he didn't pedal his cycle-rickshaw between three small villages within a few miles of each other along north India's Yamuna River. Sometimes he even made trips to the ancient town of Kalpi, ten miles to the east. Ajit worked long hours six days a week to earn an income sufficient for Padma and him to start their life together.

Ajit jumped up from his sleeping mat, pulled on his dhoti and ran barefoot to the chilly courtyard. He looked around frantically. "Where are you?"

"Over here. By the trees."

Padma was on the other side of their hut near a stand of mango trees. Half-eaten fruit lay scattered on the ground. He looked up into dense foliage to see three large monkeys in the big tree and two young ones in one of the four smaller ones. They were brazenly picking the precious fruit, even though it wasn't ripe enough to eat and still bitter in taste. After one or two bites, the chattering thieves tossed the uneaten remains to the ground.

"Ajit! They're destroying our mangoes!" she cried as he ran towards her.

"Get back! These monkeys can be vicious," he said, as he looked around the courtyard desperately, as if trying to decide what to do.

Suddenly, he opened the gate and rushed to the path in front of their hut and grabbed a handful of stones, then quickly returned to where Padma was yelling up into the maze of branches. Ajit began throwing the stones, first at the smaller monkeys, then at the three adults. His barrage drove the two little ones over the nearby wall. The large male, however, even though struck forcefully in the chest, scrambled to the lowest limb and screeched loudly while making threatening lunges toward Ajit. The two females joined in with piercing shrieks and violently shook fruit-laden branches within their reach.

Not wanting to further enrage the nasty invaders, Ajit and Padma ceased their effort to drive them away and retreated to the hut. They had heard too many stories of monkeys ferociously defending their food when challenged.

"What can we do?" Padma asked in a panicked voice. "They'll destroy the whole crop if we don't stop them. I need the mangoes to make chutney. For cooking . . . and to sell in the market."

"I know. We have to do something. But what?" Ajit replied.

"Why don't you ask Mr. Sharma? Maybe he'll know," Padma suggested.

"Good idea. I'll go see him now. He's always up early. Stay here. But don't go back out there," he said, hastily putting on a clean shirt.

Mr. Ashok Sharma, a Brahmin of some small but not insignificant wealth, was acknowledged as the village headman. He readily dispensed advice and rulings with fairness and thoughtfulness to all who sought them.

As Ajit walked briskly along a dirt track towards the center of the village, the threat the monkeys presented to his and Padma's well-being was foremost in his mind. He reflected on how important it was to save the mango crop Padma was counting on. His thoughts then strayed to how wonderful the past two months with Padma had been. How, after the hectic wedding days, he was finally able to take his new wife to the home he'd created for her. The hut was located at the edge of their small hamlet. Both their families had lived in this village, or in one of the other two within walking distance, for as long as could be remembered. Ajit had inherited the abandoned dwelling, along with an adjacent small plot of farmland, from an uncle who died a year before the wedding, about the same time Padma's sickly mother and much older father had died. Ajit spent what money he'd managed to accumulate as a cycle-rickshaw-walla, and some borrowed from another uncle, to make the repairs necessary to render the hut habitable.

The plot next to the hut had been fallow for several years. Ajit intended to rent it to one of the village farmers since he had no intention of working it himself. The rental income, although not a great amount, would be a welcome supplement to his rickshaw earnings.

Ajit had taken possession of his father's cycle-rickshaw after his father was killed six years earlier when a transport truck careened out of control on the narrow highway to Kalpi and crashed into the tea stand where he'd stopped. for a break. The three-wheeled cycle had a carriage seat that accommodated two passengers and had a rack on the rear for packages. As a child, Ajit had learned to maintain it in perfect working condition and had repainted it several times. He always knew it would be his someday and that he would willingly follow his father's path.

"Ajit! Where're you going in such a hurry?" a voice cried out from the doorway of a small hut.

Ajit recognized the greeting from his cousin, Sunil, his mother's sister's son. But being in a hurry, he didn't stop to talk. "I'll see you later. I have to see Mr. Sharma," he yelled over his shoulder as he picked up his pace, leaving Sunil standing in the courtyard wondering what the rush was all about. Sunil, who lived in Kanpur, a large city fifty miles to the northeast, was visiting his mother, who'd remained in the village after her husband died a few years earlier.

Continuing towards Mr. Sharma's hut-house, Ajit recalled that the first thing Padma did when entering their own hut for the first time was to inspect the inside pantry area. The space where she would store the pots and pans her mother had given her, the water jug, and herbs and spices she'd collected over the past months. Satisfied with the solid cabinet, the wall hooks and two sturdy shelves, she went out to the fire pit in the hard-packed dirt courtyard. The curved iron rod for hanging pots above a dung-fire was perfectly serviceable. The stones around the pit were exactly as they should be.

Padma had been pleased with the quality of it all, and with the thoughtfulness of Ajit's efforts, especially because of her passion for cooking. In fact, even though she was the youngest in her family, she was considered the best cook among four sisters their mother had taught culinary skills that were so important to an Indian wife. Padma was not only proud of her knowledge, but also of the vast store of recipes she had committed to memory. This treasure included the supposedly secret family recipe for a spicy chili-mango chutney that she'd cajoled from her maternal grandmother before her death.

"You're up early for a Sunday," a man squatting in his door-yard next to a plastic bucket and dousing water over his body yelled as Ajit hurried past.

"Problem with monkeys stealing our mangoes," Ajit shouted in return, continuing on without further comment.

A few minutes later Ajit approached the respected village elder where he sat in the early-morning sunshine, cross-legged on a rope-strung cot, in his courtyard. He was wrapped in a soft cotton shawl and held a glass of steaming sweetened chai.

"Good morning, Ajit. Come sit with me."

Ajit had profound respect for Mr. Sharma. After his father was killed, he often went to him for advice, which the old man gave generously.

After a respectful Namaste greeting, Ajit wasted no time in getting to the point of his visit.

"Sir. Monkeys have invaded our mango trees and won't leave when I yell and throw stones. Our crop will be devastated by the time it ripens. What can we do?"

After a few moments of silence, Mr. Sharma responded. "You have only a few options. One, you could borrow Mr. Kahn's shotgun. If you shoot one of them the others will leave and never return. But, as you know, such an action would be against our belief of not taking the life of a living being. Not even a pesky monkey. The monkey god, Lord Hanuman, would most likely be angry. An outcome you should not risk."

"I agree, Mr. Sharmaji. We don't want to kill one of them. Is there anything else you can suggest?" Ajit asked anxiously.

"Or you could leave them alone and share your crop with them. They too are children of the Lord," Mr. Sharma answered.

"But sir . . . with only a small income from my rickshaw, we need to harvest as much of the mango crop as we can."

"I understand," Mr. Sharma replied sympathetically. He allowed a few minutes to pass in silence. "There *is* another possibility," he finally said.

"What?"

"Use nature to balance nature."

"How can we do that?" Ajit responded with a puzzled look on his face.

"You could let the monkey's enemy do the job for you."

"But, Mr. Sharmaji, monkeys have no enemy but man."

Mr. Sharma answered at once, "That is not true. Through all the ages, monkeys have been prey to one especially fierce predator. Their most feared enemy. The Indian leopard."

"How could we use such a wild beast for our own purpose?" Ajit asked, immediately skeptical of Mr. Sharma's surprising proposal.

"I will make inquiries. Come back later with Padma. Ask her to bring some of her delicious samosas. Perhaps I will find a way to protect your mangoes from those thieving pests."

On his way back to his hut and Padma, Ajit was having a difficult time grasping what Mr. Sharma suggested. Trying to imagine how he and Padma could take possession of a leopard and use it to keep the monkeys away from the mango trees. But his thoughts kept returning to how important the fruit was to Padma. How she was counting on it to help build a better future for them. How he would do anything to help her in that regard. How much he loved her.

Ajit and Padma had known each other since childhood, playing together in dusty village lanes and laboring in surrounding agricultural fields. Although she'd grown into an attractive and sought-after young woman, Padma had managed to avoid an early arranged marriage. She also persisted in her schooling, believing she was destined for a life beyond that of just having children, cooking and fieldwork. After eight years of primary school in their own village, both she and Ajit completed the first two years at the government-run secondary school in Kalpi. Ajit had to drop out to support his mother after his father's death, but Padma, as well as his cousin Sunil, took and passed the qualifying exams and completed the final two years. But rather than pursue higher education, as she could have, Padma chose to remain in the village to help her aging parents and someday make a life there with Ajit.

Padma had loved Ajit from an early age, as he did her. Because of their mutual stubbornness and acquiescing parents, they'd been able to fly in the face of tradition and manage a love-marriage rather than let their families choose their mates. They were determined to make a secure future together; one they knew they would have to create themselves, however they could in a rapidly changing India.

Later that afternoon, Padma and Ajit were sitting with Mr. Sharma's on a woven mat on the floor of his-house, chatting and sharing sweet chai and Padma's freshly-made vegetable samosas. After Ajit and Padma politely declined Mrs. Sharma's offer of a third refill of chai, Mr. Sharma turned to the issue of monkeys in the mango trees.

"The wildlife station in Surmat is closing and is required to dispose of their animals, including a young Indian leopard. She is quite tame and accustomed to being with people. They have to find a home for her, or else release her into Gir National Park. She would have no chance of survival and would either starve or be shot by some Gujarati farmer intent on protecting his cows from attack by a hungry leopard. My cousin's son Ambar is assistant to the director. The director is willing to arrange for our village to take her. She would have to live under your protection. I am confident that she would drive the monkeys away. They have a natural fear of leopards."

Ajit and Padma were astonished by Mr. Sharma's suggestion, even though he'd mentioned the possibility when Ajit visited him that morning. But never in their wildest imaginings had they thought he would actually arrange such a thing. That they might become keepers of a leopard. But, since they both believed the mangoes could be a stepping stone to a better future, they knew what they had to do.

Glancing at Padma and acknowledging her brief nod, Ajit answered in an unwavering voice. "We'll take the leopard. Tell them to bring her next Sunday."

Padma abruptly rose from where she'd been sitting, collected the tray of remaining samosas and offered them to Mrs. Sharma, then thanked Mr. Sharma for his help and Mrs. Sharma for the tea.

"Come, Ajit, we have a lot to do," she said excitedly, glancing back at him as she hurried through the open doorway and walked off at a fast pace towards the far edge of the village where their hut was located.

Ajit jumped to his feet and scurried to catch up with her.

Monkeys in the Mango Trees

The Attack

"**Y**ou're late. Where've you been?" Padma asked, not attempting to disguise her concern.

"I went to Kalpi for that fencing," Ajit said, pointing at a rusty tangle of wire strapped to his rickshaw. "It was in a trash pile at a construction site."

"I'll bring your dinner and get your tools," Padma said approvingly as she surveyed Ajit's treasure, then hurried towards the hut when he began to unload the mangled mess.

Since agreeing to adopt the leopard Mr. Sharma had arranged for them, Ajit had accumulated enough discarded materials to build the framework of an enclosure large enough for a big cat to get the exercise it needed. A covered shelter along its back wall would allow the leopard to stretch out to its full length and sleep protected from the elements. Now Ajit could finish the pen before the leopard was to be delivered two days later.

While Ajit worked his rickshaw during the day and labored early mornings and late each night to build the enclosure, Padma had been doing her best to drive off the monkeys every time they invaded her trees. Although somewhat successful, there was still additional loss of mangoes. Her shouts and rock throwing were effective with the younger monkeys, but the bigger ones usually ignored her, especially the vicious male. Each day as the mangoes ripened a little more, her frustration grew, her patience decreased, and she became anxious to have the leopard to unleash on the thieving primates.

Mr. Sharma showed up at Ajit and Padma's walled courtyard the following Sunday afternoon. A garishly-painted flatbed truck pulled up behind him; *Surmat Wildlife Station* was painted on the driver-side door. A cage containing a young leopard was tied down to the bed. Wooden crates stacked next to it were secured with thick ropes. The driver blasted the horn three times, cut the engine, and climbed down to the dirt track. Two young men got out and joined him.

Ajit and Padma greeted Mr. Sharma, then acknowledged the driver and his helpers. Ajit led them to the enclosure he'd completed that morning. The driver examined it closely and nodded his approval. Padma looked at Ajit and smiled. Noticing movement, she looked up into the largest of the mango trees. It was the male monkey, his big head cocked to one side. He was staring at the cage on the back of the truck.

The workers lugged the wooden crates into the courtyard. Then they removed the ropes holding the cage in place and lifted it down to the ground. The leopard twisted and turned in the confining closure, snarling and striking out with quick slashes at the two men as they half-carried, half-dragged it to the gate of Ajit's pen where they lined up the two openings.

"She's usually not this wild. Must be upset or scared about being taken away from the refuge where she's lived all her life," the driver said. On his signal, one man raised the cage gate and the other prodded the leopard with a stick. The leopard growled once at the man, then, paying no further attention to him, treaded cautiously into its new home. After one of the men pulled the cage away and closed the pen gate, the animal stood unmoving, surveying its surroundings. It glanced at the driver, then at Ajit, then Padma, on whom its scrutiny remained for a longer time. Finally, it went over to the roofed shelter, sniffed the ground, and lay down, then attentively watched its captors go about their business.

"What's that collar around her neck?" Padma asked.

"An electronic one. We're going to install a wire along the top of your wall. She'll get a shock if she gets close to it. But don't worry, she'll still be able to climb the trees and chase away the monkeys."

"What's in those boxes?" she then asked, pointing at the row of crates stacked along the wall.

"Enough canned goat meat for three months. After that, you'll have to provide her food yourself."

After the wire was anchored atop the courtyard wall, and a section buried in the dirt under the gate, the two helpers dug a trench out to a pole that stood beside the path in front of Ajit's property. They carefully spliced the perimeter wire to the single electric line delivering power to some of the village's four dozen huts. The driver inspected everything they'd done, then looked at Mr. Sharma and nodded approval.

Their work completed, the driver gave Ajit a pamphlet titled, "Facts About Leopards," then got into the truck with the two others. He slowly backed along the path, with Mr. Sharma leading the way.

Ajit opened the pamphlet, scanned it briefly, then read a few sentences out loud.

The leopard is the smallest of the four "big cats," the others being the tiger, lion, and jaguar. The Indian leopard is widely distributed on the subcontinent and subsists on small hoofed animals, monkeys, rodents, and birds.

He turned to the next page.

The biggest threat to leopards is illegal poaching. Skins and body parts are smuggled mainly to China.

After he finished reading, Ajit and Padma stood admiring the leopard stretched out on the tree limb which Ajit had placed in the pen. One end was planted solidly in the ground, the other reached upward, then horizontally, about four feet above the dirt floor. Unblinking yellow eyes stared back at them, seemingly without menace. The beast's velvety spotted coat glimmered in rich colors. Luminous, even in the soft winter sunlight.

"She's beautiful, isn't she?" Padma said softly.

"Yes. She is. And trust me; poachers will never get their hands on her," Ajit said with conviction.

A moment later she said, "Do you think I should go into the cage and make friends with her? I could take in her food."

"No! Not yet. Maybe in a few weeks. Let her come to know and trust you first. I'll feed her this time. I'll just slip it inside the gate."

"No!" Padma replied emphatically. "I'll feed her. She won't hurt me. Get some meat from one of those boxes and put it in a pan."

Seeing the determination on her face and detecting it in her

voice, Ajit didn't argue.

A few minutes later, Ajit opened the wire-mesh gate and Padma cautiously stepped in and edged over to a plastic pan full of water that sat on the ground near the entry. She stooped and placed the metal bowl containing the meat next to it, all the while humming the soothing melody of a song her mother often sang while cooking over her courtyard fire pit or tending to her four young daughters. The leopard watched her every move, but remained on the limb, as still as a rock. Padma then stood to her full height, paused a moment, and smiled at the leopard. Resuming the ancient lullaby, she then left through the doorway that Ajit held open for her.

Ajit replaced the padlock on the gate and they went into their hut. It was time for Padma to prepare their own meal.

The next day being Monday, Ajit returned to his cycle-rickshaw work and Padma to her household responsibilities, which now included care and feeding of the leopard. Over the following weeks, she developed a fondness for the animal. Her feeding, watering, and cleaning became acts of love rather than unpleasant chores. The leopard must have sensed Padma's feelings and quickly accepted her presence in the pen, eventually even letting Padma scratch behind her ears and rub her belly. As time went on, the big cat learned to obey the verbal and hand-signal instructions Padma was teaching her. She would lie down, leap onto the tree limb, even growl and snarl on command. A strong bond gradually developed between the leopard and Padma, far different from anything Padma had experienced growing up with her family's bullocks and goats. This was something special.

One Sunday morning a few months later, after Ajit had bathed and eaten his breakfast, Padma called him over to the pen where she stood observing the leopard.

"What do you want?" Ajit asked. "I have to clean the rickshaw and replace some spokes in one of the rear wheels. They were damaged when a load of lumber fell off a handcart."

"Yes, I know. You told me that yesterday. But first we have to decide about the leopard."

"Decide what? Everything you're doing is perfect. What is there to decide?" he asked, puzzled by her statement.

"It's time to let her have free run of the courtyard," Padma answered.

"Are you sure? If she escaped, it would be disastrous. We would be in a lot of trouble. Anyway, the monkeys haven't returned."

"That's not true!" Padma said adamantly "Three of the monkeys came back yesterday and ate more of the mangoes. They're not afraid of her since she's always in the pen. Even when she snarled at them they didn't leave."

Ajit sighed with resignation. "Okay. I'll talk to Mr. Sharma. We have to find out how he would feel about this."

"I'll go with you," Padma said in no uncertain tone. "Wait! One more thing," she added as he started to walk away. "We have to give her a name. She has become my friend. All of my friends have names."

"Padma! Are you becoming obsessed with this wild animal? She is not your child. She needs only food and water to do her job. Not a name."

With a beguiling smile, Padma said, "We'll call her Nagina. Now go fix your spokes and hurry back. I need your help. We're going to make a batch of chutney to sell in the market."

It was late that afternoon when Ajit rang the cow bell on the post next to Mr. Sharma's front door.

"Hello, Ajit. Namaste, Padma," Mr. Sharma said, then invited them inside. His wife greeted them and offered tea.

"I made these samosas today, and this chili-mango chutney is from a fresh batch," Padma said, offering the gifts to Mrs. Sharma.

After chai and samosas, accompanied by the chutney, Ajit broached the purpose of their visit. He explained Padma's desire to give the leopard free rein of their courtyard, and how the monkeys had learned there was no danger since she was confined to the pen, and that they had recently returned.

When Ajit finished, Mr. Sharma addressed Padma directly. "Are you sure of the leopard's control by the electric barrier? And that she will not escape? That she is no danger to you and Ajit?"

Padma answered immediately. "Yes. The driver who brought her said she is accustomed to the collar, and that it prevented her from leaving her area at the wildlife station. She obeys me. I trust her. Yes. I am sure."

"Then you have my permission," Mr. Sharma said without hesitation.

"Thank you," Padma replied happily.

As Ajit and Padma prepared to leave, Mrs. Sharma said, "Your chili-mango chutney is unlike any chutney I've ever tasted. It's delicious. It has such an unusual combination of spices. Some I don't even recognize. Now I understand why you're determined to protect your mangoes."

"Thank you, Mrs. Sharma. And as far as the monkeys are concerned, Nagina will do her job," Padma replied confidently as she followed Ajit out the door.

The sun was disappearing into the western horizon as Ajit and Padma approached their walled yard. Much to their surprise, the gate stood open. A flatbed truck stood nearby with an empty cage strapped to its bed.

"Ajit!" Padma screamed. "Poachers are after Nagina!"

"Stay here. I'll see who they are," Ajit yelled as he rushed into the courtyard.

"Get away from there!" Ajit shouted when he saw two men forcing open the door to the leopard's pen. He grabbed a mattock leaning against the courtyard wall as he raced towards them.

One of the intruders, raising a stout stick over his head, turned to face Ajit's onrush, but not soon enough. Ajit swung the mattock and struck the man in the shoulder hard enough to drive him to the ground. Blood gushed from a deep gash. The rope the poacher had been holding in his other hand flew through the air.

With Ajit off balance from his just-in-time lunge to reach the poacher, the other man was able to smash the butt of a rifle into the side of his head. Ajit instantly dropped onto the hard-packed dirt.

From beyond the open gate where Ajit had commanded her to stay, Padma watched in horror as her husband fell to the ground where he remained unmoving, apparently lifeless.

Monkeys in the Mango Trees

Challenges

"**N**agina!" Padma yelled as she rushed through the open courtyard gate. As she ran towards the pen she screamed as loud as she could to distract the poacher with the gun so he wouldn't further harm Ajit, who was still lying motionless on the ground, and also to alert their neighbors.

When she reached the pen, the burly man raised his rifle to bludgeon her. But as he started to swing the gun, the leopard sprang through the open door and onto his back. The startled thief cried out in agony and tried to shake himself free from the razor-like claws digging deep into his body. He dropped the weapon and crashed onto the hard ground with the snarling leopard maintaining its unyielding grasp, her glistening fangs hovering close to his neck. Padma ignored the man's cries for mercy. Nagina held him down, but did no more than that, as if awaiting instruction from Padma.

At that same instant, two neighbors came running into the courtyard. "What's happening?" one of them yelled.

"These thieves were trying to steal Nagina," Padma cried out from where she knelt next to her husband. "Ajit is hurt. He needs help."

"I'll get Mr. Sharma and the doctor," the other neighbor shouted, running off at once.

While Padma attended Ajit, the remaining neighbor retrieved the rope, cut off a length and tied up the poacher Ajit struck down with the mattock. Then he picked up the rifle and leaned it against the courtyard wall.

"What about this other one?" the neighbor asked, returning to Padma and glancing at the bleeding and whimpering poacher restrained by the leopard.

"Tie his legs. Then I'll call off Nagina. Be ready to tie his hands."

The neighbor did as instructed.

"Nagina," Padma said in a calming voice, placing her hand firmly on the leopard's shoulder. "Come." She coaxed the big cat hesitantly off the subdued poacher and into the pen, then closed the gate.

A few minutes later, with Nagina settled and both poachers securely tied, Padma brought water from the hut and cleaned the laceration on Ajit's head. Then Mr. Sharma and the other neighbor arrived. When Mr. Sharma knelt next to Padma, Ajit's eyes fluttered open.

"Dr. Chopra's on his way. I sent for the police, as well," Mr. Sharma said.

Ajit mumbled something unintelligible then slipped back into unconsciousness.

Mr. Sharma turned to Padma. "What happened?"

"Nagina attacked the poacher. I'm not sure why. I screamed and ran to help Ajit. Maybe I yelled her name. I'm not sure. It happened so fast, it's a blur. She must have wanted to protect us."

"It's a good thing, no matter what the reason," Mr. Sharma replied, glancing at the leopard that was standing unmoving at the gate staring intently at Ajit.

By the next afternoon, Ajit had recovered enough to sit up on his sleeping mat. Dizzy and unsteady, he tried to stand. The walls of the hut swirled around him in the dim light.

"Dr. Chopra said you have a concussion and have to rest until you're strong again," Padma told him, easing him back down. She also described how the police took the poachers and their truck away, and that they'd been looking for them for the past year.

"They praised your bravery, but said you were foolish to attack them alone," she added, her scolding softened by an approving smile. "The police were going to take Nagina because of what she did to the poacher, but Mr. Sharma wouldn't let them."

"When did you teach Nagina to attack? Mr. Sharma told me about it when he came by a while ago," Ajit said.

"Never."

They stared at each other in silence for a moment, then Padma said, "She saved our lives, didn't she?"

"Yes, she did," Ajit responded. "We must never forget that."

But as happy as Ajit was with the capture of the poachers, and that Nagina had protected Padma and was not taken away by the police, he was worried about the loss of income since he was too weak to work.

"We need money. What can we do?"

Padma was ready with a solution. "Don't worry. I'm going to sell our chutney at the Kalpi market tomorrow. We have extra mangoes to sell, too. Sunil can haul the chutney and mangoes in your rickshaw. He's in the village this weekend, and he'll take two days off from his job. We'll leave at dawn and be back before dark."

"When I'm in Kalpi I will visit your mother, too. And see your sister. They know you were hurt, but will be okay," Padma added.

Ajit's half-hearted objections to Padma's reliance on Sunil, based on a long-held dislike of his cousin, were easily overcome by the soundness of her plan and the force of her determination.

Even though they were the same age, Ajit and Sunil had not been close as children. Sunil was highly intelligent and a grade ahead of Ajit in school but was ambitious and conniving. He was always willing to do whatever it took to get what he wanted. Ajit also suspected that Sunil had wanted to marry Padma. Sunil's bitterness was obvious when she chose Ajit instead. He and Padma were happy that Sunil lived in Kanpur where he worked as a manager in his uncle's chain of neighborhood markets and rarely came to the village to visit his mother. Ajit knew beyond certainty that Padma loved only him and accepted Sunil's help simply because she needed it.

The next evening, Ajit was roused from a restless sleep by Padma calling from the courtyard.

"We're back."

Ajit tried to get up but fell back onto the pallet as the room spun in slow circles.

Padma rushed into the hut, her dusty sari fluttering behind her. "We sold everything! Here. Look at the money," she said proudly, loosening the drawstring and emptying her cloth bag onto the floor next to the sleeping pad. Quickly adding up the coins and bills, they realized it was more than Ajit made in a whole week as a rickshaw walla.

Padma was bursting with excitement. "The chef from a big hotel was our first customer. After he tried the chutney, he bought twelve jars, but demanded a discount. He said it was the best he'd ever tasted and will serve it in their restaurant. He said we could promote it as an organic gourmet product, whatever that means. All the mangoes sold, as well. But the profit is better from the chutney. From now on, we'll use all the mangoes for chutney. We'll buy them from our neighbors to have enough for larger batches."

Ajit felt overwhelmed by Padma's unrestrained enthusiasm and was confused by her sudden transformation into a budding businesswoman. He knew of no other woman in the village, or in the ones close by, who spoke like that. *Is it right that a woman should be so bold, so involved in business, so . . . equal?*

Not wanting to dampen Padma's passion, but unsure of what course of action to take, he said, "We have to talk to Mr. Sharma about this. Your plan will involve the whole village. We'll need his permission."

Two days later Ajit was strong enough to walk with Padma to Mr. Sharma's. After the usual greetings and servings of tea, Ajit described Padma's idea. Padma provided the answers to Mr. Sharma's questions about the details of her plan.

When Ajit and Padma finished describing their proposition, Mr. Sharma looked at his wife with a perplexed expression. Saying nothing, Mrs. Sharma simply bobbed her head a little and smiled at Padma.

Mr. Sharma then said, "Ajit, will you allow Padma to do what she proposes?"

Having spent the preceding two days listening to Padma, he was now a convert to her cause. "Yes," he said without hesitation.

Thus, with Ajit's formal endorsement of his wife's proposal, there in a mud-walled hut-house in a small farming village beside one of the holiest rivers in India, the Indian Leopard Chutney Company was born. The name was chosen by Padma on the spur of the moment. It acknowledged how the company came into being because of the fear that a band of raucous mango-stealing monkeys had of a young female Indian leopard that had been rescued from certain death by a forward-looking newly-wed couple.

With Mr. Sharma's approval and support, it didn't take long for Padma and Ajit's fervor to infect their neighbors. Soon, everyone in the three villages who could was selling their fruit, hot peppers and herbs to them. But as important as the chutney recipe and availability of fresh ingredients were, there was Padma's growing business skill, along with Ajit's unwavering support and newly-discovered organizational talents, that not only allowed the business to survive the unavoidable ups and downs of a start-up, but also flourish.

Within twelve months, they'd found space in their own village where Ajit, through trial and error and with much help from others in the villages, and using a builder from Kanpur, managed construction of a processing and packaging shed. The company gradually added half a dozen employees, including Sunil, who took charge of sales, and with time developed a successful marketing program. The years working in his uncle's markets in Kanpur had given him familiarity with the food business, a factor that convinced Padma and Ajit, although reluctantly, that his experience would benefit the company. New products based on guarded family recipes contributed by other women in the villages extended their product line and produced increased revenues and profits. In the beginning they invested every rupee back into the business, allowing them to produce and sell a little more with each batch. Like successful entrepreneurs the world over, they refused to give in to failures, learned from their mistakes, and steadily improved operations and financial success.

In a mere three years the Indian Leopard brand was recognized throughout the country. Although the products were more expensive than those of competitors, they were better tasting, and . . . organic. The target for the Indian Leopard products was higher-income earners comprising India's growing middle class. They could easily afford the prices and were receptive to the budding organic food movement. Others were swayed by the company's policy regarding poaching of India's wild animals; five percent of profits were dedicated to enforcement of anti-poaching laws.

But growth of their business was not without problems. With time, expanding demand for their products became an increasingly difficult challenge, especially when complications began to outnumber solutions. Frustrations came to a head one morning as the couple was on their way to the production shed, where Padma also had her office.

Ajit broached the subject when he said, "We're operating 24 hours a day, seven days a week, and we still can't fill all the orders. We'll have to expand soon."

"I know. Many of our best customers are complaining. We're so far behind. What can we tell them?" Padma said.

"I don't know. But there's no way to increase production here in the village. Anyway, we need to be in a city, maybe Kanpur or Lucknow. Closer to suppliers, and transportation. Better water and electrical service. But that would be like starting over," Ajit replied, a hint of despondency in his voice.

"Ajit, I don't know what to do."

They walked on in silence, overcome by the implications of the decisions they faced, and by the magnitude of the problems.

As they continued along the path winding beside the river, Padma thought of personal concerns as well. Thoughts she'd put aside during the past couple years. What should they do with the money they were accumulating? Did they want to continue putting all their time and energy into the company? What about the family they had planned? Would there be time for raising children? What did they want out of life? Were they happy? What about Nagina's future?

It was with such thoughts occupying her mind later that morning, after spending frustrating hours responding to complaints about delivery delays, that Padma went to find Ajit. Spotting him with a mechanic working on one of the pieces of equipment, she approached and motioned him away.

"What are we going to do about a new facility?" she said, the exasperation of needing to make a decision evident in the tone of her question.

"I told you, I don't know. Production problems are taking every minute of my time. We're behind schedule because this labeling machine keeps breaking down. Last week it was the—"

"Ajit! We have to decide! We can't keep putting it off," she said heatedly, ignoring his frustration.

Ajit's irritation turned to anger. "Padma! Leave me alone. I have to get this line going. We'll talk tonight. Go back to your papers and phone calls!"

Padma was shocked by Ajit's response. He'd never spoken to her like that before. *What's happening to us?* she wondered as she walked slowly back to her little office space in a far corner of the big shed. When she opened the door, Sunil was there waiting for her.

Monkeys in the Mango Trees

Revelations

"What are you doing in here?" Padma exclaimed when she discovered Sunil sitting at her desk.

"Oh . . . Padma," he said awkwardly, then put down the papers he was leafing through. "I was, uh . . . looking for the list of shops that responded to our ad for more sales outlets. But I came to talk to you about my marketing plan. We need more sales. You know . . . make more money?" he said, fumbling for words as he rose from the chair.

Padma was not placated by his response. "You shouldn't be here. Not looking through my papers, either. Now leave," Padma said as she stepped into the little room.

"You're right. I shouldn't have come into your office when you weren't here. But before I go, there's something I need to say," he blurted out, remaining where he stood.

Without waiting for her response, he forged ahead. "I can tell that you and Ajit are no longer happy like you used to be. I knew someday you'd see what a fool he is. That you would eventually realize it is me you should've married. I've always loved you, even when we were in school in Kalpi. Can't you see that it's me you deserve, not a lowly rickshaw walla? I have more to offer. More education, more business experience."

Padma was shocked. "Get out of here!" she screamed. "I don't want to hear any more of your nonsense."

Sunil, at a loss what to say, with a look of despair quickly replacing the conviction of a moment before, dashed past her and stormed through the open doorway.

Padma sat trembling in her chair, trying to comprehend what Sunil had said. She was appalled by his delusions. By his suggestion that she might think of Ajit as a failure. She loved Ajit unconditionally. He was her rock—her life. But as she calmed, she considered what Sunil might have observed to encourage such boldness. Was it true that she and Ajit appeared unhappy together? She needed to think. To find answers to questions far more important than how to sell more chutney.

Suddenly she thought of Nagina. She yearned for the calming effect the placid animal had on her: The feel of her velvety fur. She missed the sense of well-being she had when she rested her head on the leopard's chest and absorbed the resonance of her deep purring sounds. Padma sprang up, closed and locked the office door, left the production shed and started towards their hut.

Along the path, Padma reflected on how, over the past three years, she had neglected Nagina. How she took for granted that Nagina kept the monkeys away. How the freedom for Nagina to roam unfettered in their courtyard drove the thieving monkey family away from the entire village. She was overcome with the realization of how much she needed her.

Soon Padma reached their courtyard and opened the gate.

"Nagina! Where are you?"

At the sound of her mistress's voice, the leopard bounded through the open door of her pen and came running. Nagina rubbed against Padma's sari, circling around, arching her back, purring her familiar greeting.

"Come," Padma said softly. She buried her hand in the big cat's soft coat and led the way to the shade of the big mango tree. She sat down on a mat of woven reeds with her back against the courtyard wall. Nagina stretched out beside her.

Her thoughts drifted back over the past few years. She saw how her focus had shifted away from her husband, her duties to her sisters and his mother, even away from Nagina. She'd focused her energies on creating their chutney company. She succeeded in attaining her goal, but her success hadn't brought satisfaction she thought it would. As she sat in the stillness of her thoughts, she came to understand that what she'd achieved, though it was against monumental odds and an accomplishment to be proud of, wasn't worth the possibility of losing Ajit's love or separation from her family. That those were the enduring values she must cherish and hold on to at all cost. Then, in a flash of clarity, the solution came to her.

"Nagina!" The leopard's eyes flashed open and her ears pricked up, jolted by Padma's sudden outburst. "The answer is so obvious, so simple. I can hardly wait to tell Ajit."

It was late that night when Ajit returned to their hut after long hours with the mechanic to get the labeling machine going. He left his sandals by the door and collapsed wearily onto their new wool Kashmiri carpet spread over the clean-swept dirt floor. Padma was waiting with his favorite yogurt drink, sweet mango lassi. She quickly started a fresh batch of naan on a cast iron griddle resting on the gas ring while a covered platter of chicken masala and potato-cauliflower curry warmed in the coals of the courtyard fire pit where she still preferred to cook, even though Ajit had recently installed the gas burner inside the hut.

"After you have eaten and rested, will you feel like talking?" Padma asked with a soft voice from across the room where she was finishing the naan.

"Yes. There are things we need to discuss. I've been thinking about what our life has become, especially after I got so angry with you today. But first, some food."

Soon Padma brought over their masala and curry, along with a cloth-covered basket of naan and bowls of rice and dal. She sat down on the carpet across from him. They ate in silence, both hungry because of the lateness of the hour. When they were finished eating and the metal dishes and cups removed, Padma began. She went directly to the heart of the matter, as was her way.

"I think we should sell the company."

A smile lit up Ajit's face. "I'm happy to hear you say that. Happy because I don't want to continue living as we have these past two years. For me, there has been little pleasure. And it saddens me to see how you've changed, so concerned with bigger and bigger production lots and getting higher and higher prices for more and more products. We have more money than we could ever have imagined. But we go through each day as though we have to make more. Why are we working like slaves when we don't have to?"

Padma listened attentively as Ajit continued to express his feelings, at times nodding her head in agreement. When he finished, she spoke.

"Today, after I got so angry with you for no reason other than my own frustration, I realized that we had to change everything or risk losing each other." She paused to wipe away the tears running down her cheeks. "There is nothing I want more than to be with you. I want our old life back. And I want to start our family."

Ajit took her hand in his, pulled her close and put his other arm around her. Her sobs were only partially muted when she laid her head on his chest.

The following months passed in a flurry of activity, all directed toward selling the Indian Leopard Chutney Company. Ajit's success in restarting the production line soon eliminated the pressure of late deliveries. Additional sources of ingredients to meet increased product demand were confirmed; revenues continued to climb. Ajit and Padma's extraordinary efforts resulted in a smoothly operating and profitable company that would be highly attractive to potential buyers.

But even with this busy schedule, Padma found time each day to visit Nagina. The strength she'd gained from their closeness allowed her to face the business challenges she had relished in the past but had come to resent. Padma also put off meeting with Sunil about new marketing plans. In fact, she avoided him as much as possible. Neither he nor she mentioned his outburst and criticism of Ajit, as if it had been temporary madness on his part. As far as Padma, she didn't want Ajit to know about Sunil's behavior for fear of what Ajit might do to him and the troubles that would bring them.

By the following summer, Padma and Ajit felt that the time was nearing to set the plan they'd formulated in motion, but not revealed to anyone else.

"Before we take the final step, we have to talk with Mr. Sharma. We'll need his approval for such a major change," Ajit said as they walked alongside the river one morning on their way to the production shed.

Upon hearing Ajit's revelation that the chutney company was to be sold, Mr. Sharma was unable to hide his surprise. "But the village now depends on the company for its livelihood," he said, shedding his usual serene demeanor and prematurely interrupting Ajit's presentation.

"We would do nothing to harm the village," Padma exclaimed passionately before Ajit could continue. "What we propose will be better for everyone than just selling mangoes or working on a production line. Some of the workers have even said they would like to get back to their fields—that too many are untended and have gone to weeds. After all, Mr. Sharma, sir. We are a village of farmers, aren't we?"

Over the ensuing hour Padma and Ajit explained how the funds from selling the company would be used to convert a portion of the chutney shed into a modern school for the three villages. How the college in Kalpi would provide teachers as part of their teacher training program and pay for supplies and utilities. A small student fee would help defray expenses. They described how the rest of the space would be developed as a state-of-the-art medical clinic and funded on a continuing basis by the C. S. Maharaj Medical University in Lucknow, which would use it as a rural healthcare delivery training center for their interns. They would also offer courses in healthcare support positions for local people. And Dr. Chopra would have his own outpatient clinic in the facility. Ajit and Padma mapped out the entire project, step by step. They explained that only a portion of the proceeds from the sale of the chutney company would be required for the renovation, the rest would be placed in a trust to contribute to ongoing operation costs.

"This is our gift to the village that made our success possible in the first place," Ajit concluded with obvious pride.

Overwhelmed by the audacity and magnitude of their proposal, Mr. Sharma was nearly speechless, although not quite. "I must talk to the other elders about this. Come back tomorrow evening and I will give you an answer."

The next evening Ajit and Padma found Mr. Sharma surrounded by

four village elders. Mrs. Sharma sat next to him.

"We agree that your proposal will help our children and improve the lives of all the villagers. You have our permission to carry on with your plan, and also our deepest gratitude," Mr. Sharma said in a rather formal, albeit emotional, tone, then smiled broadly.

After answering questions about timing and logistics, and many cups of tea, Ajit and Padma were finally able to take their leave. As they approached the door, Mrs. Sharma, who had been silent until this moment, called out to Padma. "Do you have any of the Leopard's chili-mango chutney you could spare?"

Padma turned and smiled. "I'll bring a jar tomorrow. And I'll make sure you never run out. I will always make enough for ourselves and our friends. My grandmother would never forgive me if I failed to do that."

On their way back to their hut, Ajit broached a topic that had been on his mind since their decision to sell. "What about your grandmother's secret chutney recipe? That's the cornerstone of our business and will have to be sold along with all the other recipes. Are you willing to do that?"

A hint of a smile was the only indication Padma was thinking about Ajit's question. Finally, she answered. "Nānī would be pleased that her recipe will be responsible for the good things this sale will make possible. Think of it as her gift to the village."

"I am proud of what you have done, Padma."

"Thank you, my husband. That means everything to me."

Hand in hand they walked on in silence. A full moon suspended in a cloudless sky illuminated the path that meandered through the ancient village back to their modest hut. To Nagina, and to their life together.

Monkeys in the Mango Trees

Now What?

With Mr. Sharma's approval, Padma and Ajit proceeded with their plan to divest the company. Their first step was to inform their employees and assure them they would be rewarded for their loyalty and hard work. Some were disappointed, especially Sunil, while most accepted the obvious reality that the company had outgrown its present situation. In fact, the majority were happy to return to their lives as farmers, and to their traditional way of life.

A week after Padma and Ajit's announcement, a few hints regarding the intended sale were intentionally leaked by their lawyer, Mr. Mahendra Patel. This "rumor" resulted in a rush of inquiries from specialty food companies that had felt the impact of Padma's brilliant business strategy on their own revenues. Soon, a half-dozen competitors anxious to add the Indian Leopard brand to their own product lines were requesting meetings.

During this period, as interest in purchasing the company mounted, Sunil paid an unexpected visit to Ajit, who was working in the production shed. Forgoing preliminary pleasantries, he immediately began angrily accusing Ajit of betrayal by selling the business—betrayal of Sunil himself, of the company's other employees, of the whole village.

"You have no right to destroy my career, my income, my life. Are you going to let your crazy wife undo everything I created? I should be the one to run this company. You should give the business to me since you and Padma are unable to manage it any longer!" Sunil's anger approached hysteria as his harangue grew more frantic.

Ajit was caught off guard by Sunil's accusations, then realized that his cousin might be on the verge of a nervous breakdown. "Stop!" Ajit said forcefully. Sunil, shocked by Ajit's strong response, quieted momentarily. Ajit took advantage of the lull and placed his arm around Sunil's shoulder, then guided him to a nearby bench. "Sit with me and tell me your concerns."

Suddenly Sunil began crying uncontrollably. "What will I do? This is all I have. Please, don't take it away from me," he blurted out between sobs.

"Sunil. We're family. We'll look out for your best interests. And you can return to your old job with your uncle."

Abruptly, Sunil stopped crying, stared at Ajit for a moment, then jumped up and screamed, "I don't want to go back to that. I want to keep this one. I hate you! I hate Padma! I won't let you do this!" He turned his back to Ajit, stormed out of the shed and disappeared in the blinding sunlight.

That evening, sitting in their hut with Padma, Ajit described Sunil's behavior and shared his suspicion that his cousin might be on the verge of mental collapse. "We'll have to look after him when the company's sold. I know he has some problem and gets too excited sometimes. That he loses his temper too often. But he's smart—and a hard worker. And he doesn't want to work for his uncle anymore. Maybe there'll be a job for him in the clinic or the school," Ajit said.

"Maybe," Padma replied unenthusiastically. "Let's see how things turn out. We shouldn't make promises we wouldn't want to keep."

The pending sale of India's premier chutney brand was a major event in the specialty foods sector. The news spread fast and sparked a fierce bidding war. Initial offers were even greater than Ajit and Padma had anticipated. The morning on which the winning bid was to be announced, they sat in Padma's office talking by phone with their lawyer and the transfer agent, preparing for the conference call with the four top bidders that was scheduled to start soon.

Just before the teleconference was to start, the office door crashed open. Sunil stood in the doorway. "I won't let you do this," he cried out. His words slurred. His glazed eyes flitted back and forth from Ajit to Padma. He reeked of cheap whiskey. "It should be mine! My work made it what it is."

On the other end of the phone, Mr. Patel realized what was happening at once; Ajit had previously mentioned Sunil's discontent. The lawyer immediately used another phone to call Mr. Sharma.

Padma stood and took a step toward Sunil. "There's no need for anger. We know how valuable you've been. We'll reward you for everything you've done."

Before Sunil had a chance to respond, Padma noticed Mr. Sharma through the open door. He was on the other side of the production line and she shouted, "Mr. Sharma, come and join us. Sunil is here."

The rage on Sunil's face turned into an expression of confusion. When he turned to look behind him, Ajit quickly took him firmly by the arm and led him out of the office. "Mr. Sharma wants to talk to you, Sunil."

They met Mr. Sharma walking toward them.

"Is everything all right? Mr. Patel called," Mr. Sharma said.

"Everything is under control. Sunil wanted to tell us about his concerns. That's all," Ajit said.

"Sunil, let's go to my hut for some tea. I want to know what your plans are now that the chutney company is going away. I've heard your uncle wants you to run his new store in Lucknow."

Ajit stood for a moment and watched the two walk away with Mr. Sharma holding Sunil's arm to steady his cousin's wavering steps. He then returned to Padma's office when he heard the phone's speaker suddenly come to life. Mr. Patel's voice was loud and clear. "We're still here and heard everything. Should we postpone the call?"

Although a little surprised, since in the excitement she'd forgotten about the open phone line, Padma responded immediately. "No. Sunil just left with Mr. Sharma. We're ready."

The sale went as smoothly as anyone could have hoped. Patel and the agent deftly negotiated the sale price substantially higher than they had anticipated. Padma and Ajit were relieved that the ordeal was finally over and that everything worked out so well.

Especially, even though the bulk of the proceeds were for the clinic and school, that Padma had managed to allocate sufficient funds for the Gir National Park to establish The Nagina Indian Leopards Sanctuary. She believed she owed that much to her own leopard.

Taking everything into consideration, the stress and occasional strife that Padma and Ajit had endured, the near-breakdown of Sunil, even loss of the famous secret chili-chutney recipe, in the end, the Indian Leopard Chutney Company adventure was a grand success. Especially for Padma. She had shown that a poor village woman could achieve great things and was exceptionally proud of that.

Five years later . . .

Padma entered the courtyard of their clay-brick four-room house that stood where their former hut had, holding the hand of her two-year-old daughter, Lata. Her four-year-old son, Naveen, trailed close behind. She 'd collected the two from the day-care center that served the clinic and school located in the remodeled shed that used to house the chutney company. Nagina heard them coming and was waiting. Lata rushed ahead as Padma swung the entry gate closed and set the latch in place.

"Hold still, Little Princess," Padma said as she lifted her daughter up and set her onto the leopard's back. The little girl's laughter echoed off the courtyard walls. Naveen jumped up and down in anticipation of his turn. Lata held tightly to the thick fur around Nagina's neck as the leopard loped over to the palm frond-covered back corner where the children played in shade while Padma prepared their lunch.

After bringing Naveen to join his sister, Nagina stretched out on the cool earth next to Lata, who was playing with the animals Ajit had carved from scrap wood he'd collected. Naveen was nearby, driving a little home-made wooden truck along roads he'd

31

made in the dirt. While Padma was in the house preparing their meal, the leopard watched the two children with unwavering attentiveness.

At that same moment, Ajit was pedaling his cycle-rickshaw along the road to Kalpi, hurrying to a pickup request he'd received on his new cell phone. After the school was up and running and Ajit was no longer involved in its construction, he'd returned to his rickshaw business. It was only two days a week and wasn't for the money. "I miss my friends, being out in the community, the life of the street," he had said to Padma at the time.

At first, Padma was surprised by Ajit's decision to return to his old occupation, but with time came to understand why he had. After all, who was she to pass judgment on anyone who followed their heart's desires? Ajit also kept his volunteer job at the school where he taught bicycle maintenance and repair. "Bicycles are an important kind of transportation and someone has to keep them working," he told anyone who asked about the class.

When Ajit wasn't working his rickshaw, or teaching bicycle repair, he was with their two children. Most days, with Naveen alongside and Lata in her cradle, or crawling around in the soft earth, Ajit worked in Padma's herb garden, It included a variety of culinary and medicinal plants. After the school and clinic became operational, Padma had more free time and began studying Ayurvedic medicine formulas recorded in her maternal grandmother's journals. Her grandmother, who'd died several years earlier, was not only the source of the chili-mango chutney recipe but had also been a healer famous for her salves, powders, and extracts. It was well-known that she 'd wanted her granddaughter Padma to follow in her footsteps.

Padma did as her grandmother had wanted, but her herb garden was only part of it. She also spent time at the village clinic with Dr. Chopra, where traditional Ayurvedic treatments were combined with western medicine, a practice Dr. Chopra enthusiastically endorsed. They were both impressed with the efficacy of her treatments and natural medicines. Gradually, local villagers, and even people from Kalpi and more distant locations, sought her healing powers. She felt fulfilled, even privileged, by keeping her grandmother's work alive.

Padma was about to pick up the tray with the children's lunch when she heard a piercing scream. She knew at once it was Naveen and rushed out the door.

"What's wrong?" she yelled as she ran towards the crying boy who was holding out his arm, swelling and discoloration already forming around two puncture wounds on his hand. She saw a snake clamped in Nagina's mouth, thrashing around wildly, then going limp when the leopard shook it more forcefully. Padma swept up the child, ran back to the house, and laid him on a pallet. With lightning speed, she grabbed a cloth and tied a tourniquet tightly around his arm. She then auto-dialed Dr. Chopra at the clinic.

"A Russell's viper struck Naveen. Bring the antiserum as fast as possible. Hurry!"

Then she ran to the kitchen cabinet for a jar of a salve her grandmother had mixed for snakebite and applied it liberally to the wound. Padma had seen its effect on one of the village men years ago and hoped it retained its potency. With these things done, she called Ajit.

Within minutes Dr. Chopra burst into the room and injected the antiserum into one of the boy's vein. "It's good that you used the salve to extract some of the venom. Normally, it would have killed a small child in the time it took me to get here."

A little later, when Naveen had calmed, and Padma sat next to him holding a cool cloth to his forehead, Dr. Chopra addressed her in a quiet voice. "I knew your grandmother well and trusted her treatments. They were based on thousands of years of Vedic teachings. I sent many patients to her over the years. You are fortunate to have been chosen by her to carry on the tradition. It's a precious gift, and you must use it well."

The mood was suddenly interrupted when Ajit burst through the door, out of breath from racing home after Padma's call.

"How is he?" Ajit said urgently, kneeling next to Padma and looking closely at his beloved son.

Dr. Chopra answered in his doctorly manner. "He'll be fine. His arm will be swollen and sore for a while, but he'll live."

The worry drained from Ajit's face and his eyes teared up. He put his arm around Padma and pulled her close. They watched Naveen until he fell asleep.

That evening, after a light meal when both children were asleep, Padma sat next to Ajit and took hold of his hand. "There's something
I need to talk to you about."

"What?" Ajit said, a worried look appearing on his face.

"Promise you won't be angry?"

"I promise. Unless it's something I *should* be angry about."

She waited a moment, then continued.

"I'm thinking about starting an Ayurvedic medicine business."

After a short moment, Ajit, struggling to squelch a smile, said, "Oh, is that all? I was afraid it was going to be a serious *problem* of some kind."

"I *am* serious," she said earnestly, ignoring his undisguised flippancy. 'Will you help me?"

"Hmm . . . we did all right with your grandmother's chutney. I suppose we could do just as well with her medicines." He took hold of her hand. "Of course, I'll help. I'll have to take a couple of years off from my rickshaw business and put it back in storage. After all, I *do* have to keep it safe for Naveen. He'll need it in about ten years if he decides to carry on the family tradition."

"Thank you, my love. I couldn't do it without you."

"Sure you could. It just wouldn't be as much fun. Or as easy. So, what's the first step?" he asked, pulling her closer.

"This," she answered, kissing him passionately.

Elly's Story

By Linda Burke

My name is Elly. Carl and Linda, the people who take care of me, gave me that name when we met. I don't remember much about my life before that, but I think my dad was of German Shepard decent. He was a traveling man, if you know what I mean. My Mom was the "looker" in the family. She had blond fur and long floppy ears like a retriever. I have my mom's coloring and my dad's green eyes and long nose. My early years are a blur. I learned a few human words like sit, shake, dinner time, and learned to do my business outside in the weeds. But I never got the hang of coming to people when they called my name. It was too much fun to roam free and sniff all those good smells.

That roaming thing got me in trouble one time when I ended up in somebody's yard. The people had a couple round-headed kids who liked to make a lot of noise and a real cute black and white collie dog. I didn't have a collar, so they kept me for a few days, but couldn't find my owners. After a few days I was ready to roam again, but they had me fenced in. I felt like a prisoner, but at least I got two square meals a day.

One day Carl and Linda came to visit. They made a fuss over me, then went off to the side to whisper something. Next thing I knew, I was riding in their car. We came to their little farm, and the first thing they did was give me a bath. I didn't mind because my fur was matted and very dirty. I felt better after I was dry again. I sniffed around the house and it seemed okay. They even had a nice soft bed for me.

My roaming urge was pretty strong. Every time they opened the door I would bolt and disappear for a while. It was fun exploring. Our one neighbor had a horse. I thought I was tall! I stand as high as five Chihuahuas stacked together, but I only came up to the horse's knees. They also had a Doberman named Wally. He was a big sissy. He barked and carried on every time I came to visit but wouldn't leave his porch. That was okay. I don't like to play with other dogs anyway. The neighbor would hurry out and shut the gate, then Carl would come over and put a leash on me to lead me home. Carl and Linda took me for lots of walks. They put a strange contraption over my nose. It would pinch if I pulled too hard, but after a while we understood each other. Eventually I quit bolting out the door because I knew I would be treated well.

One-day Carl came home with two donkeys. I was a little intimidated by their size (about the size of the horse). They named the old one Elly Mae, and the daughter was Josie. They stayed in the fenced-in pasture and ate lots of grass. In the early morning they both would bray as loud as they could. It woke all of us up. All they wanted was some hay! Not even a juicy bone! Sometimes deer hopped over the fence and grazed with the donkeys. The donkeys didn't mind unless the deer got too close. I kept my distance too because Josie had a wicked kick.

A few months later Carl brought home a huge jack. A jack is a male donkey. He was kept in a separate field for a while, but then Carl let him into the same field as Elly Mae and Josie. Carl was hoping that Jack and Josie would have a little romance and produce a little one. Jack gave a new meaning to hot to trot! He spent the day chasing Elly Mae and Josie. Elly Mae wanted nothing to do with him and kept kicking him in the chest. Josie did some kicking too, but eventually let him have his way with her. I didn't understand their courtship rituals. That kicking bit was terrible. Before my owners took me to the vet for a little operation, I had some good times with the boys in the neighborhood, but we didn't do any kicking. The sad part about Jack is that the next day he keeled over and died. Carl thought he might have gotten a blood clot from all the kicking. Everyone felt bad. But what do you do with a dead donkey? Luckily, the neighbor had a backhoe and came the next day. He dug a huge hole to bury Jack.

As luck would have it, Josie did become pregnant and eleven months later had a little jack. He was brown like Josie and had spindly legs. He was just about my size. Carl helped Josie because she was a bit confused about what to do with this little creature. She soon got the hang of it and he grew into a jack the size of Josie. Carl had a great time with the three donkeys. He brushed them, sprayed them to keep the flies off, gave them special treats like carrots and apples, and cleaned their hooves. Elly Mae protested vigorously when he touched her feet. She wouldn't stand still and had to be tied to the fence. I doubt if it hurt her feet. Maybe she was ticklish. When their hooves needed to be trimmed Carl found an Amish farrier who did a great job. One day the young Amish man and his sweetheart came down to the farm in his buggy. They had a picnic by the river, then gave Linda a ride in their buggy. Linda said the seat was hard and the ride bumpy and preferred a car, but horse and buggy is the only way the Amish travel.

My next story will be about Pebo and the Guinea hens.

Love, Elly

Pebo and Company

By Linda Burk

I thought our family was complete with three donkeys and myself, but Carl decided we needed a few more animals if it were going to be a real farm. He took his old pickup and headed for the farm auction. I was a little suspicious when he arrived home with a strange looking animal in the back of the truck. He was taller than the donkeys and seemed quite snobbish; he held his head high and looked down his nose at us. He just stood there chewing his cud. I heard Carl and Linda talking about it. His name was Pebo and Carl called it a llama. Carl and Linda watch the National Geographic channel on Television a lot, so I know llamas are considered beasts of burden. They are easily led by their owners and carry all kinds of things to the markets. Pebo wasn't one to take easily to a halter and he sure wasn't very cooperative. His way of telling people to bug off was to spit some nasty stuff at them. Luckily, Carl had a wide-brimmed hat that he bought on a trip to Peru, so the stuff didn't get in his eyes. Pebo ignored the donkeys, and vice-versa, and I stayed out of his way because he was a wicked kicker. I've heard that some people use llamas to guard their sheep from coyotes and bobcats.

Pebo preferred the nicely manicured lawns of our neighbors and spent most of his time there. He was sad and lonely. His job was being a stud before his owners sold him at the auction. Carl decided Pebo needed some companions, but our farm was too small for more llamas. So, he sold Pebo to a farmer who had several female llamas, a few buffalo, and a couple ostriches. We drove by once in a while and Pebo looked content among his new friends.

The next thing I knew, we had a pen full of chickens and a little rooster who crowed when he felt like it (which was often). The silly creature was always showing off for the girls. Next, Carl brought home three Guinea hens. They were strange looking birds. Kind of looked like gray footballs with legs. I would go up and sniff around the pen, but the Guinea hens would get all excited, and the noise was deafening! It hurt my ears! I got away from them in a hurry. I can see why some farmers prefer Guinea hens over watch dogs because they never let up when strangers come around. Carl is the only one who can get close to them. Linda also keeps her distance.

In the summer, I like to go wading in the river. I was never much of a swimmer, even when Carl tried to coax me into deep water. The water was cold, and I preferred to splash along the shore. They often went for rides in their canoe. They let me sit in the middle. I never tried to jump out. We liked to drift along on a quiet afternoon, watching great blue herons strolling along the shore, bald eagles soaring overhead, and Canada geese circling overhead and landing on the river.

The only time we avoided the river was Fourth of July. For some strange reason, crazy people set off things that made loud bangs like gun shots or bombs. The sparks flew everywhere. Linda and Carl hated the noise and chaos, so we stayed away. The other noisy time was duck- hunting season. Looney people built a brown hut that looked like the trees around it. They dressed up in these brown costumes to match the hut and sat in it until the geese flew over. Then they would pull out their guns; BAM! BAM! Geese would squawk and run into each other trying to get way from the noise and shots. I wanted to bite those mean people! One goose was really smart and hid in our barn. Linda loved birds so she had a good chuckle over that goose, and never gave away her hiding place.

Sometimes it rained so much that the river flooded almost to our road. We knew not to get too near because we could see that the water was very swift. We saw boat docks, huge logs, outhouses, and garbage floating by. Carl wondered if it all made its way to the Chesapeake Bay. The neighbors living beyond our place always parked their cars along the field when it rained heavily and walked our back field to their houses because the road dipped down and sometimes flooded during bad storms. One house flooded to the second floor. What a mess! That didn't happen too often, so they took it in stride and the neighbors helped clean up afterward.

One of the neighbors had eleven cats. Cats and I don't see eye to eye. They roam the fields and kill birds, which always made Carl mad. When he spotted a cat, he sent me out to chase it away. I never caught one, but I had a good time trying. Sometimes they lost some cats to coyotes. They were strange people and blamed the missing cats on the neighbor. There was a feud going on most of the time. The cat owners would put their garbage on a neighbor's property and play loud music all night long. Why people don't get along is beyond me. If I have a problem with another dog, we just have a tussle and that's the end of it, unless it's one of those small yappy dogs. They aren't worth my trouble.

One of my favorite times of the year is winter. The snow is deep sometimes. On the Winter Solstice a bunch of people would come over and sit around a big bonfire. It was so cozy and there was a great fire to cook hot dogs. I always managed to get one or two. It was a good life and always something happening, but Carl and Linda were restless and looking for some new adventures. That might be another story.

Love, Elly

Engineer

By Mizeta Moon

Some guys hated the run across the prairie states. Me? I loved it. Signed up for it every time I could. Looked forward to another midnight roll across flat lands under wide-open skies. Loved to hear steel on steel; clattering, shrieking, and humming the miles away.

When the boilers were perking at just the right temperature, you could feel the surge of steam being taken up by giant wheels roaring over beams laid down by the sweat of many brows. Plunging into the night as the stars cartwheeled in constantly shifting patterns and all else faded into the past while our headlight lit the way ahead.

Releasing the shriek of the whistle at obscure crossings. Awakening some, comforting others who knew that our passing time was the same every night. We pulsed and creaked. We clanged and banged. Hissed and bellowed as we pierced the darkness with our mighty thrust. The wealth of a country lay in our care and we stewards of the rails always rose to the task.

Some of us more than others, but me, I always loved my job. Dropping cargo in the dead of night at lonely way-stations providing a lifeline to rural communities. Delivering an object that adorned or sat under a Christmas tree later. Or became an anniversary present and evoked tears of joy. Keeping commerce alive and bellies full. Keeping the mail moving and expanding the American horizon. It was wonderful knowing that I touched thousands of people's lives without one of them knowing my name. Just a man doing a job with his face turned into the wind and feeling the thrill of motion. Our lives are moments, and those were some of my finest. As homage to the bounty I was bestowed, I composed a ditty to sing to my iron steed as it charged across the prairie.

Choo-choo train. Choo-choo train. I'm driving you tonight. Diving straight into the moon as it rises past the corn. Straight into tomorrow. Straight into the heart; of a sleeping nation and of a shooting star.

In the Beginning

By Howard Schneider

DATE: 13.8 billion BCE
LOCATION: Undisclosed; too dark to know.

The primordial soup came alive with quiet chatter and occasional subdued laughter. A low hum droned in the background.

Suddenly a new presence was sensed. Except for the faint humming, there was instant silence.

"Greetings, colleagues," the new presence projected. "It's been a while."

"Yeah. Like a couple billion years," came a distant snarky reply.

"I think you'll see that the wait was worth it," the new presence continued, ignoring the interruption. "I'm pleased to announce that we can finally move ahead with project 14B. As you can sense from the vibratory energy surrounding us, and that barely perceptible buzz you feel as much as hear, our research guys have at long-last succeeded in creating the perfect basic particle. At least that's what they claim. Shortly before this get-together, I approved release of a test sample. Although you may not be able to tell from such a short exposure, this version is actually everything we hoped it would be. They've come up with a real doozy. They even built in properties they call gravity and anti-gravity, kinda sorta like attraction and repulsion, only a lot more complicated. As far as I'm concerned, it's exactly what we need. No doubt about it. We're good to go."

The collective gasps and murmurs of consent, bolstered by the absence of objections, signaled to the boss that the experiment about to be set in motion garnered broad support. Not that such agreement was actually required. But if things didn't work out, it would be nice to be able to spread the blame around.

"Any questions?" the boss tossed out.

"What's the next step?" came from somewhere.

"The next step will be my okay for broad-scale release of the particles. Time will take care of the rest."

"What do you think will happen?" came from somewhere else.

"We're not exactly sure about the actual details. Calculations are still preliminary, and the equations include quite a few variables, although we do have some rough ideas. The particles might actually exist in variant states and could eventually combine to form larger units of complex matter. At some point, sufficient mass could be attained so that larger entities would be drawn together by gravitational forces to create huge collections of solids and gases. The math guys tell me that since infinity is so vast, we could end up with billions of what they're calling universes. It's like this infinity thing doesn't ever end. I mean, think about it. That's really big. Anyway, according to the equations, these universes would be made up of billions of galaxies, which consist of trillions of these weird formations they've termed stars. Gigantic fiery balls of matter and energy. Pretty wild, huh?"

"Wow! That sounds like a lot to keep track of. Do you think we gods might be biting off more than we can chew?" a far-away voice resounded.

The boss replied without hesitation. "I don't think so. We're not exactly amateurs, you know. But we'll just have to wait and see, won't we? It would be pretty boring if we knew all the answers ahead of time."

"What's the particle called? Does it have a name?" someone else asked.

"No name yet. At this early stage the research team can't decide whether the particles are matter or energy. They refuse to give it a name until they figure that out. I tell ya—sometimes those research guys drive me nuts."

"One more question. Not exactly related to 14B, but I'm curious to know if you were ever able to figure out where all of us came from. Like, who made us? Remember? That came up at our last get-together."

"Uh . . . yeah. Right. As far as I know, the guys in Public Relations are still working on that. I'll definitely check into it and let you know as soon as they come up with something. Okay. If there are no more questions, let's get on with the show," the boss said.

"Just one more question," someone else said. "What will our jobs be in this project?"

"Is that you, Lucifer? I'd recognize your voice anywhere. We're still working on that. I'll send a memo around as soon as the committee develops a definitive plan. Right now, we've got bigger things to think about. As of this instant, we're on our way."

She then pressed a big red button that said, 'To Start, Press Here.'

The Climb

By Mizeta Moon

We were laboring our way up the rutted path to the peak of Mt. Scott. My pair of oxen were well-fed and strong, but the grade was steep, and their breathing was strained. Should we make the top I would be jubilant.

An erosion formed by spring rains resulted in a gully that was difficult to traverse. I urged my team on and they bulled their way forward in response. They were fearless when I needed their strength and I told them so as we navigated the next stretch of the path. I felt nothing could stop us, but hadn't counted on the perversity of nature.

Within sight of our destination, four fallen trees blocked further progress. My team stood snorting and breathing heavily before an obstruction they couldn't surmount. I looked for an alternate way but saw nothing promising. I would have to chop my way through or turn around.

For hours I toiled with my axe. Grew weary, felt thirst, but persevered beyond exhaustion. When I'd finally cleared a pathway through, I wept with relief. Tiredly climbing behind the reins, I urged my stalwart companions upward, and they leaned mightily into the yoke. The path grew even more treacherous as we neared the property I'd bought from the land office some months before.

Just short of the peak, my oxen slowed as there was a field of small boulders ahead that they wouldn't be able to negotiate. Their eyes rolled back towards me as they silently pled to be relived from their task. I called for a halt and assessed the situation. The meadow where I planned to build my house was less than a hundred yards away. I could carry loads across one at a time, and though it would take some time to empty my wagon, I was blessed by an abundance of it. Where we stood at the moment would provide adequate forage for my team, so there was no need to further tax their strength or harm their hooves.

I was anxious to stand at the top. Climbing from my perch, I took up my stick and tackled the daunting footing of those last yards, vowing to create a path before transferring goods. Reaching the clearing, I felt at home. I became possessed of a serenity like nothing I'd known till that moment. I walked to the edge and indulged myself with a view of sheer majesty.

Snow-capped mountains rose from miles of verdant fields. Their shoulders were laden with stately trees until reaching heights where nothing grew. Geese flew across a cerulean sky while the wind blew lacy clouds towards the horizon. At my feet the grass was lush, and a wealth of clover promised honeybees whose sweet nectar I could harvest. Dandelions would bring wine to the table and the soil would teem with a harvest my seeds would provide. My heart spilled over with joy as I gazed. The fruit I could grow and the abundance that rain would sustain were a worthy reward for the toil of our climb. There would be happiness here and time to appreciate what wonder surrounds us.

The Newsboy

By Mizeta Moon

"**P**aper lady? Latest news. Murder in Canby. Robbery in Oregon City. Best details. Only a nickel."

I nearly cried when I looked at him. Thin, ragged, shoulders quivering from the cold and rain. A woolen cap providing a canopy for eyes filled with need. A burning soulfulness lusting to survive.

"Paper?"

I'd come prepared. Knew he haunted this corner. Knew the nuns I'd left him with treated him poorly instead of using my endowment to nurture him and school him for success. There was little I could do about that but withdraw my financial support, and then where would he go?

"I don't need a paper, but would you like to have dinner with me? My car is just around the corner. I won't hurt you. No need to be afraid."

"Of you, lady? Sure . . . I could use a bite."

"This is a keen car. I never rode on leather seats before. What kind is it?"

"It's a Duesenberg. I'm glad you like it. Sit back. Enjoy the ride. Dinner is a few miles away."

I abandoned him shortly after his birth because my husband said he'd kill us both if I kept him. Said he owned me now that we'd robbed our way from Chicago to Boise, then coasted into Portland in a car we'd stolen in Missoula that was dying every moment. When the car refused to go any further, we walked to a hotel and started a whole new life.

My husband was smart. He turned our ill-gotten gains into a

string of auto dealerships and eventually bought us a house on the slope of Mt. Tabor. We became absolutely necessary to a successful party and our wealth increased in volume as we became scions of Portland society. The only thing poisoning my soul was that year we'd spent in the hotel where my son had been born and I'd been forced to abandon him to save his life.

"This food is really swell. You don't need a kid do ya? A guy could get used to this."

Once again, my heart was breaking. How long could I live this lie? How much could a mother deny? How could I leave him on the curb and drive away?

"I'm glad you like it. I've arranged for you to take some home with you. I hope the nuns have room in their refrigerator."

"If they don't, I'll share it with the other kids. This is really nice, lady. Thanks a bunch."

The drive back was over too swiftly. I'd given him a coat at the restaurant. Nothing fancy that bigger kids would take away. Warm, and waterproof. Wind resistant when the gorge howled and raged.

I'd given him a little money, but not enough to brag about and find himself in trouble over. When I idled to a stop, he gathered his bundle of papers from the floor and reached for the door handle.

"Wait! I meant to give you this." I said with more passion than I'd felt in a long time.

It was a locket with a picture of me.

"Call me mom when you're lonely," I whispered, as he clasped my gift and stepped into the rain.

Lost

By Howard Schneider

If you want to have some fun, try this. Randomly open a dictionary (I personally use a Random House Webster's College Dictionary but use whatever you want; it makes no difference for this particular exercise). Now that you've opened it, close your eyes and stab your finger onto the page. Either side. Left or right. Again, it makes no difference. Once your finger is resting on its landing spot, open your eyes and look at the word. Now, write a story about it. No matter what the word is, just start writing. Pretty easy, huh?

Assuming the validity of my supposition, I followed my own instructions and landed on the word "run". You know what happened? I was instantly overwhelmed with the magnitude of the challenge. Why? Because there were 87 separate meanings of the verb and 41 of the noun. I'd be writing for the next year and a half if I took on all these possibilities. That's not what I had in mind.

"So," I said to myself, "Start over. Make another choice." I did. This time the word picked by my random stab was "lost." Much better, easier to deal with. At least compared to "run."

The word "lost," with its eleven meanings, is one of those words frequently used to convey a reality that often signifies the darker side of life. Grammatically, it can serve as either an adjective or a verb, and in either case often represents situations fraught with difficulty, regret, or sadness. For example: the man lost his temper when he was unable to find his lost keys. Verb and adjective in the same sentence, both conveying the possibility of unhappy outcomes.

Think further about its varied uses as an adjective and as a describer. Common examples: "lost friends, lost children, lost money, lost prize, a lost chance, a lost battle, lost ships, the lost look of a man in trouble." Worst of all, a "lost life." Then there were the "Lost Tribes of Israel," and the "Lost Generation," both of which are examples of major historical significance.

On the other hand, the word can be used to describe a state of being, as in "lost in thought," or "lost in sorrow." Or perhaps, "lost in the delirious joy of love," or "lost in the pursuit of truth—or happiness." All interesting possibilities. All rich source material for stories.

Then there's the verb; its use in this way is flexible as well. How about, "He lost his way," or "lost his job," or even worse, "she lost her mind? And don't forget, "men lost in battle," as opposed to the equally significant but less emotional "lost battle." Big difference between adjective and verb. Use both forms in a story to create lots of conflict and tension.

But enough of this grammar theory. What about some concrete examples of personal encounters with lost? I myself can think of no time when I have actually been really lost. That is, using the word in the sense of not knowing where I was. Actually, that's not *quite* true. There was that one time when I got lost on a high mountain in a blinding snowstorm and nearly died. But that's a tale for another time, and actually not all that interesting. Just another "lost mountain climber" tale. There're too many of those already.

On the other hand, when in grade school, I frequently got bad report card grades for "not paying attention," meaning, most likely, that I was "lost in a daydream." That doesn't surprise me as I look back at what kind of kid I was, often traveling down the highway of my own imagination, much more enticing than reciting multiplication tables for the umpteenth time.

But on a personal level, a much scarier form of "lost" was when my little brother actually really did get lost, as in, "Where's Jerry? He was here a little while ago." That was a reoccurring scenario. Jerry would just get lost in his own adventures and disappear. Once, after searching the surrounding neighborhoods, I found him hours later, pulling our ugly little dog Pudgy in his red wagon along Buckeye Road, miles from home, happy as could be, jabbering away at Pudgy as if nothing were amiss. But as far as he was concerned, he wasn't lost, we just thought he was.

Another time, when we were spending a summer in the high-altitude, clean air of Prescott, Arizona, to counteract Jerry's asthma, he and his little-girl playmate who lived in the trailer next to ours, hiked into the forest adjoining the property and didn't return. There were no answers to the loud calls of the searchers, which by late afternoon included most of the trailer park inhabitants as well as three sheriff's deputies. But then, as dark settled in, a beat up station wagon pulled up in front of the trailer park's office. A bearded old man and his wife got out and opened the back doors of the big Oldsmobile to allow the two little kids to spill out. It seemed that Jerry and Janie had gotten lost, walked out of the woods the wrong way, and ended up miles away on the other side of Prescott. Jerry had knocked on the door of the first house they came to and told the woman they were lost, where they lived, and asked for a ride home. That time "lost" turned out not to be so bad at all.

So, as far as the possibilities of "lost" are concerned, let's hope that for all of us it's more of those "lost in the satisfaction of story making" than the "lost in sorrow" kinds.

Elly's Next Adventure

By Linda Burk

My name is Elly and I loved riding in our camper van. It was like having a big doghouse on wheels and I could invite my people, Carl and Linda, to stay with me. We stopped at campgrounds that had a lot of people, and plenty of dogs, too. It got very noisy sometimes. The little dogs were never quiet. They always made a fuss when we walked by their campsite, but I was too dignified to do that kind of yapping. No one seemed to mind though. There was also plenty of music with people jumping up and down and twirling around. I heard Carl call it dancing. I didn't understand it, but sometimes Carl and Linda would leave me in the van and go do that twirling thing.

Sometimes we drove all day before stopping. I had plenty of pee and sniff breaks, so I was content and slept most of the time. One trip was all the way across Canada. Then Carl drove the van onto a ferry boat. It was a long ride, but I wasn't scared. Carl and Linda were excited to see a pod of Orcas close to the ferry. I think they were just big fish, but no one tried to catch them. On that trip we landed on the east side of Vancouver Island and stayed in a campground that had farm animals but no electricity. It was so hot no one slept well that night. In the morning, Carl drove to the other side of the island where we stayed in a little fishing village. It was cooler but smelled like fish. It made me drool. The next day I stayed in the van while Carl and Linda roamed a huge flower garden called Buchart Gardens. I imagined she "ooed and aahhed" and acted like a butterfly going from flower to flower. I wasn't allowed to go with them. It was probably a good thing because peeing on flowers is one of my favorite things to do.

Soon we were on a ferry boat again and landed in Washington, then Carl drove to Oregon. It was still very hot, but at least the campground had electricity, so Carl could turn on the air conditioner. On that trip we stayed in Oregon for a week. Next thing I knew, Carl and Linda were looking for a house to buy. Linda wanted a modern house, but Carl was set on a small, restored bungalow that was within walking distance of stores, restaurants, and a bus line. Linda finally agreed when she saw its large, modern kitchen and the fenced-in back yard where I could hang out. They signed a bunch of papers and off we went to Pennsylvania again.

Carl and Linda spent several months sorting out and getting rid of a bunch of stuff. One day a big truck pulled into the yard. Carl and their son, Brian, spent several days loading the truck with boxes and furniture. Then off we went in the van again. It took a week to drive across the country. We made it to Oregon the first week in October. We all had to get used to our new house. I did a lot of sniffing for a few days.

Linda and Carl didn't bring any beds, so they slept on a mattress that they had to blow up. I was happy in my crate. It took a week before the truck arrived with the furniture. I liked our new house and yard, but I am a roamer and a sniffer. One day they left the front door open. That was my chance! I ambled down the sidewalk, sniffing to my heart's content. It wasn't long before Linda was running after me. It was just too much fun, so I managed to keep about two blocks ahead of her. She tried calling my name over and over, but I was too busy sniffing to pay any attention. She finally caught up with me when some folks stopped to pet me. I never could resist a good ear rub. That was the end of my free ranging. Guess I'll leave that to the chickens. Oh well, they take me for a walk twice a day, so I have a chance to check out the messages left by the neighborhood dogs. It's a pretty cushy life in Portland. There are no donkeys threatening to kick me or loud Guinea hens, so I'm content. Carl kept the camper, and I look forward to more adventures.

Love, Elly

Bedtime Story

By Howard Schneider

"Charlotte, Honey. It's time for bed. Brush your teeth and put on your pajamas."

"Okay, Daddy. Then will you read me a story, like Mommy does?"

A few minutes later Charlotte was climbing into the sofa-bed he'd prepared for her in his office when he came into the little room. He pulled the desk chair up close and sat down.

"We had a fun today, didn't we," he said as he carefully helped her adjust the covers.

"Yes. I liked the zoo most. The monkeys are so fun to watch."

"Tomorrow we'll go on a picnic. That'll be fun, too. Then I'll take you back to your mother's by dinner-time. What story would you like me to read?"

"Janie likes a story called 'Little Red Riding Hood'. Mommy never read it to me. It's in the book I brought from home."

Her father retrieved the book from her duffle bag, found the story, and began.

Once upon a time there lived in a certain village a little country girl, the prettiest creature who was ever seen. Her mother.
. .

"Daddy? Why was she called a creature? She's not really a creature, is she?" Charlotte interrupted.

Her father looked up from the page, then said, "Hmm. . ., maybe when this story was written, which was a long time ago, creature meant little girls, too."

"Oh. . .. Okay. You can read more," Charlotte said.

Her mother was excessively fond of her; and her grandmother doted on her still more. This good woman had a little red riding hood made for her. It . . .

"Daddy. What's a riding hood?"

"A riding hood must be a cape of some kind, maybe with a hat, or with some kind of hood that's part of it."

"Did she have to ride something to wear it?"

"No, honey. I don't think Little Red Riding Hood rode a horse—or anything else," he said, a hint of impatience creeping into his voice.

"Why did her grandmother give her a riding hood if the little creature didn't ride anything? Do you think the grandmother was kind of strange?"

"Charlotte! It's just the name of a cape. Can I just get on with the story?"

"Okay, Daddy."

It suited her so well that everybody called her Little Red Riding Hood.

One day her mother, having made some cakes, said to her, "Go, my dear, and see how your grandmother is doing, for I hear she has become very ill. Take her a cake and this little pot of butter."

As she was going through the wood, she met a wolf, who . . .

"Daddy, wait! Why would her mother send the little creature girl all by herself to such a dangerous place where there would be a wolf?"

"Her mother probably didn't know there was a wolf in the forest. I'm sure she wouldn't have done that if she had known. Don't worry about it, Honey. It's just a story, not real life. Now, where was I? Oh yeah . . ."

". . . who had a very great mind to eat her up, but he dared not, because of some woodcutters working nearby in the forest. He asked her where she was going. The poor . . .

"Daddy! Can wolves talk? Do you think maybe the wolf just barked, and the little red girl thought he was talking."

"Look, Charlotte. This is a fairy tale. So just listen and enjoy it. Okay?"

"Okay . . . but it is kind of dumb that a wolf would talk like that."

"Charlotte!"

"Don't yell, Daddy. Mommy says you yell too much. She doesn't like it when you yell. I don't either. I scares me."

"I'm sorry, Honey. I won't yell anymore, okay?

"Okay."

The poor child, who did not know that it was dangerous to stay and talk to a wolf, said to him, "I am going to see my grandmother and carry her a cake and a little pot of butter from my mother."

"Daddy? Can I ask just one question? And you won't get mad?"

"What?"

"Wouldn't you think that the little girl would know that a wolf is dangerous? That it wouldn't be a good idea to tell the wolf where she was going and what she was carrying. She can't be that stupid if her mother allowed her to go alone through the woods all the way to her grandma's house, can she?"

After a brief moment of silence, her father, with great restraint, managed to say, "Charlotte, this story is just meant to be entertaining and interesting, even fun. You might enjoy it more if you just accept it as is and not be so concerned about whether it's logical or not. Understand?"

"Yes, Daddy. I'll try. You can read some more."

"Good. It's getting late and I would like to finish this story without interruptions."

He continued.

"Does she live far off?" asked the wolf.

"Oh, I say," answered Little Red Riding Hood; "it is beyond that mill you see there, at the first house in the village."

"Daddy?"

"Now what?"

"I don't think any little girl would tell a wolf where her grandmother lived. Especially one that talks. I think this is a dumb story and I don't want to hear any more. Can you find another one?"

"No! You asked for this one and you're going to listen to the rest of it. Now shut up. I'm not gonna tell you again."

Charlotte was shocked by her father's angry response and burst into tears, sobbing loudly and uncontrollably, violently rolling her head back and forth on the pillow as if she were in great pain.

"Charlotte! Stop that! You're acting like your mother. Hysterics aren't gonna get you anywhere."

With that said, her father jumped up, threw the book against the wall, and stormed out of the room, forcefully slamming the door behind him. He went directly to the kitchen, opened the freezer, and took out a half-full bottle of vodka. He didn't bother with a glass.

Back in her father's office, Charlotte stopped her tearless crying as soon as her distraught daddy left and then switched off the bedside lamp. Her big smile wouldn't be noticed in the dim light if her father happened to peek in. She drifted off to sleep composing what she would tell her mother when she returned home the next evening.

Red Socks

By Mizeta Moon

The carrier wore red socks, which was an infraction of uniform code something-or-the-other. Such regulations were buried in endless sub-sections and legalese, keeping lawyers employed and everyone else confused. After the seventh reprimand and subsequent payroll reductions, he'd quit caring about making his superiors happy. He figured that as long as the letters and parcels got delivered, his sock color was his personal choice.

One particular day, as he walked the neighborhood sidewalks, he noticed a lot of junk lying about, as if someone's garbage tipped over and was strewn by incessant wind. Of particular note was a broken tennis racket with a pink handle. Had it been whole, he would have picked it up and put it in his van. Pink was his favorite color.

In fact, under his uniform he was wearing pink panties and a frilly pink tank top over a Victoria's Secret bra. He wondered sometimes what would happen were he to be injured on the job. Would the hospital staff leak his secret to the Postal Inspector? Just in case, he always wore underwear that matched and was free of holes. A fashion faux pas when one was unconscious would be an unpardonable sin.

A woman stood peering out from the window of the next house he delivered to. Looking at her was like seeing his own face in the mirror. We could have been twins, he thought, as he walked away, dreaming about a pink peignoir he'd just had delivered by Fed-Ex he could try on when he got home.

The anticipation of that kept him mellow through the confrontation with Mrs. Miller's Rottweiler and Admiral Jenfall's admonitions about tardiness and shoddy service. The eccentricities of his mail recipients had long ago ceased to bother him. With thirty-five years on the job, he'd seen it all. Had suffered the snow and sleet. Had persevered through intolerable conditions and precarious happenstance. With retirement just around the corner, he could tell them all to go to hell.

But actually, he loved his job. Had spent most of his life hiking Portland's sidewalks and watching the seasons pass in their splendor. Had helped during a baby's birth. Had stood silently prayerful as a long-time client was lowered to the grave. Had eaten thousands of Christmas cookies without once falling ill. Had watched generations grow to adulthood and change addresses to new zip-codes. Had stood in pouring rain and been burned by sun relentlessly scorching everything in its path. Through it all, he'd delivered bills, personal letters and thousands of packages containing products from all around the world. He'd come to understand his role in the human saga and had achieved a sense of self-worth nothing could diminish.

At the end of his shift, he parked his delivery truck and dropped off everything he'd collected at the sorting room. Whistling quietly, he bid goodbye to his co-workers and noticed his supervisor once again staring at his red socks. Ignoring the man's scowl, he said "enjoy your evening, Mr. Davenport. They say we'll get rain tomorrow. Hope your wife is well."

Trivial chatter for a shallow relationship. How many times had the man tried to have him fired? Not to mind. Silky pleasure sat waiting on his porch. The delivery confirmation had beeped on his texting screen earlier.

Traffic was horrible on Stark St. He began getting anxious when the lights were out at 122nd, turning it into a half hour crawl through a four-way stop. By the time he reached his driveway he was sweating. The lure of the peignoir was singing in his veins.

Slamming the car door, he nearly ran to his porch, but was halted abruptly by the sight of an empty slab. There was no box with the little Fed-Ex tag. Nothing sat where his dream should have been. He looked and looked, then looked again, but it was nowhere to be found. He'd heard about the rash of package thefts in the Metro area but had always felt safe in his neighborhood. Now he'd been struck and was stunned to the core.

Heartbroken, he entered and stood crying in the foyer for several moments. Shuffling along, he made his way to the den and poured himself a stiff drink. Downing it, he contemplated another, but knew better. His rage was rising, and he was indignant that someone felt entitled to violate him and ruin his happiness.

He paced for the next half hour. Even thought about going to the corner market for cigarettes. He'd given them up years before but could really use one now. Think! Think! What could be done? Reporting it to the police would only document his predilection. It wouldn't bring his peignoir home. The only thing to do was to provide a substitute. He'd never done it before but had thought about it every time he passed by.

Suzie's Sexy Lingerie, the sign said. Calling him like a siren song, playing softly to his soul. Beckoning, like a candle to a moth. Did he dare give in to desperation? His skin ached for the feel of something new. Foreign. Unknown until experienced. There was no other choice.

He sat across the street in his car and peered through a brightly lit window filled with lacy bras and daring panties. A mannequin wearing spider-web hose smiled at passersby. The door discharged several shoppers carrying packages, and he knew with certainty that he had to go in or forever hunger. Tucking his face into his collar, he moved like a criminal approaching the scene of the crime.

The lights were too bright. Everything stood in stark relief to white shelving and stainless steel racks. His eyes were assaulted and overwhelmed. What did he want? The salesgirl was asking. Could she guide him to something?

He was about to flee when the miracle occurred. The answer to all his problems materialized from behind a nearby display. Mr. Davenport, in a Dior dress and Jimmy Choo high heels, walked towards him carrying a set of silicone breasts that, according to the package, were self-adhesive and very realistic.

Don't Get Involved with Crazy Strangers

By Howard Schneider

It was the first day of first grade and little Natalie was preparing to leave through the front door when her mother knelt in front of her and said in a serious tone of voice, "Don't get involved with crazy strangers. You never know what they might do. They could turn out to be dangerous."

"But what if I can't help it? What if it just happens?" Natalie asked, after thinking for a moment about her mother's instruction.

"Then you would have to make the best of it, Honey," her mother replied. "You would have to think hard about what to do and be fast and brave."

Fortunately, Natalie never encountered a situation such as her mother had warned against as she progressed carefree through grade school, high school, and college, entering adulthood as a well-adjusted, happy, and confident young woman. Marriage to a fine, upstanding man was followed by two wonderful children and confirmed her comfortable place in life. She was loved and safe and was grateful for her many blessings.

Being of an enlightened mind and generous nature, she gave willingly and lovingly of her time to the well-being and education of her children. This included the allotment of considerable time and energy to the world of books and reading. Their weekly trip to the local library was an especially important and was seldom missed.

But as fate would dictate, it was because of this routine that Natalie, for the first time in her life, was forced not only to recall, but also to utilize her mother's long-ago first-day-of-school instruction about involvement with crazy strangers. It happened so suddenly it's a wonder she was able to manage at all. But she did. Her inner strength was there when she needed it—she remembered her mother's very words when they came to her out of the past and guided her actions as if her mother were right there.

The first hint of discomfort was when she and her children went out the library's front door with the coming week's supply of books. As they stepped onto the portico, the door closing behind them, she couldn't help but notice the scruffy and bearded young man standing almost, but not quite, in their path on the wide steps leading to the parking lot. The man stared at her leeringly as she herded the children around him down to the sidewalk, following protectively close behind. Reaching the walkway, she quickly glanced back to see him still watching her, but now speaking into a cell phone as he took his first step down toward the sidewalk.

She hurried the children to her van. It was parked in the middle row of the three-row lot, pulled in front-first like everyone else. With the kids securely strapped into the rear seat, she climbed into the driver's seat and started the engine. She was anxious to get away from the lot and from the creepy man she knew had followed her. She shifted into reverse, then checked behind and on both sides—all clear. She backed up slowly, like she always did, and started the gentle turn to back into the wide aisle where she would shift to forward gear. But suddenly she heard a loud yell, followed by a barely detectable bump on the rear of the van. Startled, she immediately hit the brake and turned to look through the back window. She saw a red pickup parked close behind her on the passenger side, blocking her in place. A goatee-bearded, ball-cap-wearing man behind the steering wheel was shaking his fist at her and yelling something she couldn't understand.

That guy wasn't there a second ago, where did he come from, she wondered, checking her kids at the same time. They looked scared but said nothing. Turning back to the front and preparing to pull back into the parking spot, she was shocked to see the scruffy man from the library steps standing close to the front of the van, aggressively blocking her way. When he saw that she'd registered his presence, he started screaming, yelling that she hit him when she'd edged forward, even though she hadn't even moved yet. That's when she realized this was one of those insurance car-crash scams, and that from the looks of the two perpetrators, she and her children might be in danger. "Think hard, act fast, be brave," came to her instantly from deep in her memory bank.

Shoving the shifter to **Drive**, she moved forward and to the right, not stopping when she came up against the scruffy man, pushing him backwards and then seeing him step out of the way before being crushed into the car behind him. But it didn't end there. He rushed to her side window and began pounding on the glass with his dirty fists and screaming even louder, adding a strings of obscenities. The kids started crying, clearly frightened and worried about their mother's safety.

"It's okay kids, I'm just doing what my mother told me to do," she said calmly as she rammed the shifter into **Reverse** and started backing up, this time faster and turning sharper in order to get a little closer to the red pickup still angled behind her. Back as far as she could go, her bumper up against the front fender of the truck, she quickly switched back to **Drive** She repeated these actions without hesitation, apparently catching the two assailants off guard with her determination, quick thinking, and skilled maneuvering. Finally, she saw that she would be just barely squeeze between the front of the pickup and the car parked next to her. She did and made it into the wide aisle. She then slammed into **Drive** and took off like a bullet, leaving the two men behind ranting and raving at the fearless woman who had outfoxed them.

She could hardly wait to get back to the calm and safety of her own house and tell her husband about the close call. But, most of all, she wanted to pass on to her two children her mother's words of wisdom, fully realizing how important they turned out to be.

"Then you would have to make the best of it, Honey," Natalie remembered her mother had said. You would have to think hard about what to do. And be fast and brave."

"Thanks Mom," she said out loud.

The children stared at her in awe.

Flue Trouble

By Linda Burk

I loved the Franklin stove in our house on Tucker Street. I could open its doors and start a cozy fire to stave off the cold, windy Pennsylvania winters. Unlike open fireplaces, it was convenient to keep the doors closed when not in use to cut down on drafts and keep the ashes in the grate when I was too lazy to clean them out.

One summer morning, Brian, my twelve-year-old son, and Jeff, my ten-year-old son, and I were lounging in the living room, reading the Saturday newspaper and enjoying the peace and quiet after a hectic week at work and school. Tuffy, our cocker spaniel, was sleeping by Jeff's feet (probably dreaming of chasing a squirrel through the grass in the nearby park). Suddenly, we heard a rustling noise inside the Franklin stove.

"Damn," I said, "I forgot to close the flue after using the stove last winter." Brian and Jeff have wild imaginations and thought it was a boa constrictor or a huge rat. I shuddered, and told them that we live in the city, so I doubted it was an exotic animal. "Perhaps it's a squirrel or a bat."

I was feeling like a wimp and suggested that we wait. Maybe the creature would leave on its own. But, alas, the rustling noise continued. With much urging from Brian and Jeff, I knew I had to find the courage to open the doors and get the invader out of the stove.

Brian grabbed the broom and said he would try to shoo the creature out the door. Jeff quickly opened the door. I put on a pair of leather work gloves. Hoping it was a small animal, I slowly opened the doors to the Franklin stove. All was quiet. Jeff ran to the kitchen to find a flashlight and shined it up the chimney. I put my head in the stove (feeling like the wicked witch in the Hansel and Gretel story). Suddenly a blackbird fluttered down the chimney, grazing my ear as it flew into the living room! I screamed and bumped my head as I tried to get out of the stove.

Tuffy barked and jumped around, trying to catch the flying bird. Brian ran after it with the broom, knocking over a lamp and setting pictures on the wall swinging. Jeff tried to hold onto Tuffy. This continued for a few minutes but felt like hours. The screen door was still shut, so the bird couldn't find its way out and flew in circles leaving little white droppings everywhere.

Finally, the bird landed on the drapes. I stealthily snuck up on it and managed to grab it. It struggled, but I held on to it.

"Jeff, Open the screen door," I yelled.

I ran through the doorway and let go of the bird and it happily flew away.

The paperboy was standing on the porch with his mouth in a perfect "O". I'm sure he collects mostly money on Saturday mornings, but that day he collected a story about a crazy lady who keeps birds in her house.

Match Racer

By Mizeta Moon

Most of Willie Hopper's horses were losers. One step away from dog food or the glue factory. He lived out his days with little hope and few expectations, but transformation is what great stories are about, and in that respect, Willie Hopper fits like a glove.

Once in a while Willie could get one of his charges fit enough to win a cheap claiming race, but they were running against other long-term losers. He saddled a motley crew for a gaggle of owners who were poor and shouldn't be wasting their time and money. They chose to fancy themselves as big-time race people, however, thus Willie made a meager living training their stock to win races. Usually, these owners strutted around the facility acting overly smug and confident when they had a horse in a race. Afterwards, they couldn't be found.

Willie lived in a camper hauled on the back of a 1949 Chevy truck. Body rusty, tires worn, still running good despite all the miles and workload. Inside, his place was a ragged mess of racing forms, bridle and tack parts, beer cans and dirty clothes. When he wasn't acting as a glorified groom for a bunch of nags, he could be found flopped on his couch in front of a miniature television. He loved soaps, spaghetti westerns and any type of game show. His refrigerator held more beer than food.

This story begins when one of Willie's clients bought a horse in a claiming race and promptly shuttled it into Willie's barn for him to clean up after. One more mouth to feed, and too few purses to change Willie's financial status. The horse was named Mercury, but had revealed no wings on his hooves, and seemed no messenger of the gods. It took a while for him to discover what he had, but when the dust finally settled, Willie would claim he knew it from the first moment he laid eyes on Mercury. The truth of it was that Willie gave the horse a bath and comb, put him in a stall, and after feeding him, went back to the camper to swill beer and watch soaps.

During morning workouts, Mercury could run like a demon possessed. His fractions at every measuring point were incredible. One afternoon they were drilling Mercury over six furlongs and Willie doubted the veracity of his watch when it registered 1:07 flat. That was close to the world record for that distance. Willie immediately hoped no one had been watching.

Even with such magnificent speed, whenever Mercury was entered in a race the presence of other horses made him nervous and he ran rank time after time. He was usually last or nearly so and just wouldn't knuckle down to the business at hand. Willie secretly wished the owner would put the horse out to pasture. Oddly, right after a race, Mercury would be inordinately frisky and damn near kick the barn down. At the next scheduled exercise session, he ran fast as ever. It became obvious that the horse had a psychological problem. Willie didn't consider himself a psychiatrist, so he spent his time working with other horses who ran no better but were at least consistent at doing so.

When luck turns your way, it can come from the strangest directions. Willie's exercise boy had Mercury on the track one afternoon and another horse that was being breezed came bearing down on them. Mercury snorted, tossed his mane, and nearly unseated the rider when he took off. The two exercise boys quickly turned the situation into a laughingly contested race to the finish line. Mercury wouldn't let other horse pass, no matter how strongly the other rider urged his mount. Mercury seemed real proud of himself when he came back to the barn huffing and puffing. After being cooled down, Willie took a few minutes to inspect his charge from hoof to hoof. A thought had formed in his mind while he watched the exercise boys have a moment of fun. Normally, he would have chided the boy for working the horse too hard, but because the horse initiated the competition and did well, Willie felt obliged to be understanding. Besides, his idea could turn into a pile of money. He ought to go kiss the guys that now stood chatting amiably near the paddock. Maybe he'd slip them a bonus if things went well.

Willie decided to test his idea on horses from his own barn. That way no one would pay much attention to what he was doing. He sat in his camper drinking beer one night and ranked his horses from worst to what could reluctantly be called best. While other horses from his barn ran races, Mercury remained unraced, except for competing against the next in line from the bottom of the heap. Match racing was easy for Mercury. There was only one horse to think about, and he seldom had to eat dirt. Mercury blitzed every horse in Willie's barn. Once in a while he would run off a few lengths if the horse was particularly slow, but he preferred to make it close. He would taunt the other horse to pass him, then accelerate just enough to stay ahead of them. He seemed to have an enormous reserve of energy that gave him just enough to win without hurting himself. His cockiness was almost human in its manifestations. He strutted his stuff after every outing.

Willie was planning things but couldn't expose his idea to many people or he would never win a bet on Mercury. If too many gamblers got on the bandwagon, his coup would net meager returns. For the moment, he concerned himself with trying to get the racing secretary to set up a match race as part of an afternoon card. So far, his efforts were producing poor results, but he felt the begging would pay off in the long run.

The biggest thing the racing secretary had against Willie's idea was that Mercury had only won one official race in his life, and that was long before Willie ever saw the horse. Willie finally agreed to a hush-hush workout race against a recent winner. If Mercury could beat him, the secretary agreed to negotiate with the board and add a match race slot to the calendar if they approved. Such an event would have to be added to an existing schedule, for which programs were printed well in advance and changes were costly.

The day chosen for the workout race offered a warm sunny morning with only a whisper of wind. The contestants started from the gate with very few people aware of what was going on. At this point, their shared destiny might have gone up in flames (as many dreams do), but Mercury was to be Willie's guide to infamy. Like I said before, Willie was no great prize of a guy, and though not outright criminal, he was indeed capable of petty larceny. His angle was that the racing secretary would be obligated to keep silent about the results in order to avoid conflict of interest accusations. All Willie cared about was that the abilities of his horse would not be public knowledge before the match race. His horse's past record, and his own as a trainer, would make most people inclined to side with the competition. Such was his hope; lots of people betting against them and setting up a tasty payout at the ticket window. Mercury wore the other horse out by blazing the first half-mile, then loafed along to win by only what was needed. The final time was slow after such a brilliant start. Unimpressed, but willing to fulfill his promises, the secretary strode off without comment. Two hours later, Willie bought Mercury from the owner without mentioning the workout race or revealing his plans.

Large tracks seldom have a match race. A Triple Crown winner or another big-time horse could attract enough attention to make such an event worthwhile at the concessions and peripheral revenue sources like the gift shop, but at the betting window it mostly came out fifty-fifty, so lots of people bypassed match races. Like the track, with only one bet possible, the publics' take from betting pools, such as exactas, trifectas, and other exotics, evaporated. Because Willie ran at a small local track, they often relied on gimmicks and sponsor promotions to generate greater revenues. This led to the board's approval and the beginning of Mercury's rise into the record books.

A local beer company sponsored a day at the races that included sky divers, clowns, jugglers and the match race. A live band played Dixieland jazz at the front entrance where everyone of age got a free beer. On form, the race itself looked uninteresting. A non-winning nag against a proven winner. The competitor was a big, strapping black gelding that rippled with muscle. He was quick and known to have stamina, but his best time for six furlongs was 1:09 and two fifths seconds. Willie knew Mercury could run faster than that. His only worry was that the other horse might possess too much will for Mercury and outthink him. Intimidation is an animal trait that sorts out the weak from the strong. In horse racing the cream always rises to the top, barring accident or injury.

When they left the gate, the gelding quickly jumped on top and held the inside position. After the first quarter-mile Mercury had drawn abreast and was matching him stride for stride. After a half-mile, the gelding began to labor slightly and earned a nudge from the jockey. Mercury slowly moved ahead of them and began the taunting he'd shown other horses who thought they could beat him. The crowd, being unaware of Mercury's habit of doing just what was needed, saw them finish in 1:10 flat with Mercury a long neck ahead. He coasted in, but the gelding was spent by the time they crossed the wire. Willie was ecstatic as he collected various side bets and cashed in at the window. Had Mercury lost, our larcenous friend would have owed a lot of angry people money, as what cash he possessed had been passed through the ticket sellers' hands. After tending to Mercury's needs, Willie rounded up a few free beers that had been left sitting unopened around the grandstands. Returning to the barn and grabbing a blanket, Willie sat babbling to Mercury for hours while chugging beer. Eventually he fell asleep on a hay bale. The morning would find him sore and hung over, but happy and well-heeled.

When the county fair rolled into town, Willie put up ten thousand dollars from his winnings as challenge money to any horse that could beat Mercury one on one. The county track was a rutted oval of questionable distances, but Mercury took to it well and romped around as usual. Winning had toughened him up. His coat was shinier and his bearing more regal. Mercury beat five challengers during the running of the fair. The challenger's owner was required to put up a thousand dollars against Willie's ten. It was an easy five thousand that helped pay bills and put money down on a new pickup. Mercury got new blankets and tack and plenty of sorghum treats. They were on a roll and Willie felt great for the first time in a long time.

Using money he'd earned on side bets, Willie went to a trailer sales company and bought a state of the art horse hauler with built in sleeping quarters for either him or a groom. He rolled it into a paint shop to have it and the pickup painted the same shade of electric- green metal flake. A gaudy logo on the sides of each conveyance soon read **Magnificent Mercury the world's unbeatable horse**. A week later, Willie dumped his barns and training responsibilities on an old drunk who'd always wanted to be a trainer and embarked on an ambitious journey.

The incredible thing about luck is that it paves the way. Holes open up where there were none. Suddenly it's right there in front of you to pick up and fondle. Every little town they rolled into seemed to have something going on. A timber festival, harvest ball, wine extravaganza or something thematic. Anywhere he could draw a crowd, Willie raced Mercury against any local horse. At county fairs that already had horse racing incorporated into their program he would challenge their best and put up his ten thousand. As something of interest to their spectators, most tracks were willing to oblige if anyone took up the challenge and laid down their thousand dollars. Mercury cleaned them all out. Lots of farmers were sent home with feet shuffling, hands in pockets, and necks riding low in their collars. Some of the tracks were lightning fast and had accurate timing devices that showed Mercury was inching towards the six-furlong record of 1:06 and one-fifth seconds. Willie envisioned Mercury doing it in 1:05 flat.

Their next piece of luck was the intervention of a hungry news team. The reporters were doing due diligence at a fair and were desperately searching for something other than Elmer Lonetree's tenth winning hog to talk about. They greedily latched onto Mercury and Willie, who gave them an interview that was a combination of outright lies, truth and pipe dreams. They were thrilled to have something to feature on the morning broadcast. They ran the footage with almost no editing. Although the interviewers doubted that Mercury could live up to Willie's claims, they acted sincere and did their jobs. When their executive producer saw the tape, he smelled a big-bucks promotion that could generate a lot of fresh ad revenue. He was a horse owner himself and had a stallion in his barn that was quick and determined at six furlongs. This led to him arranging a match race at a good sized track with full media coverage. Overnight Mercury would become a star.

The man's name was Emil, so it followed naturally that his horse's name was Emil's Pride. He stood two hands taller than Mercury and was quite a bit heavier. Fit and muscular, he was an awesome sight to behold. The media was leaning towards Emil's

Pride, and made snide remarks about *Magnificent Mercury* at every opportunity. They were journalists just doing a job. They had exposed hoaxes before and expected to do so again.

There was a lot of hoopla attached to the day, and for once Willie wasn't amused by all the distractions. He usually enjoyed the can-can girls, and the hula hoop contests, but for the first time in a long time he was concerned about losing. When the horses finally took the track and the crowd focused their energy onto the trial at hand, Willie slipped into the zone of familiarity that had brought them this far unscathed. Hopefully, Mercury was feeling good and ready to conquer another foe.

Emil's pride was tough. Right from the gate the two horses ran eyeball to eyeball. Both jockeys tried bringing them to hand, but neither horse wanted to do anything but run. When they rounded the far turn and bore down the stretch, the crowd gasped at the fractions they were churning out. Nearing the finish line, Mercury moved slightly ahead and looked like a sure winner, but Emil's Pride still had a gasp left, and used it to draw even only yards from the wire. They were close enough at the end to flash the *photo finish* sign. An announcer told everyone to hold their tickets until a winner could be determined. Willie never had a doubt. He had seen the final lunge that kept Mercury ahead. Even when the jockeys eased up Mercury wouldn't let the other horse pass him.

When the results went up a collective groan could be heard. Most of the crowd had bet against Mercury. Willie cleaned up inside bets and did reasonably well at the window. The most amazing thing about the race was that the final time was only one tick away from the world record. That both horses had come so close was newsworthy and was noted within horse circles worldwide. The public declared Mercury's win a fluke and demanded a rematch. They would do so two weeks later, but Emil's Pride was still tired from the previous effort and Mercury ran away from him, not bothering to taunt and tease. A cry went out for an opponent that could put Mercury in his place.

For the next few months, Mercury destroyed his opponents on local cable. Several small networks rebroadcast the feeds, and that led to Mercury having a fan club throughout the country. Local chapters requested hoof prints in ink or clippings from his tail and mane. Willie started entertaining thoughts about dolls, t-shirts, and other souvenir merchandise. The problem with such plans was that Willie still thought like a cheap hustler and did poorly in meetings with business executives and wasn't popular with the media or racing sophisticates. Instead of helping him prosper, everyone wanted him to lose. Due to that, Willie spent most of his time doing what he was supposed to do. Pampering and caring for his bread-winner. Seldom has a horse been adored as such a godsend. Willie had money in his pockets every day instead of only some of the time.

Since Willie was such bad news among the racing elite, he ruled instead over the track maggots. Bet moochers, ticket scavengers and terminal losers that scooped up left-over food from tables and got drunk from dregs left in cocktail ice and flat beers. These people adopted Willie as their hero. When Willie was in a generous mood he would spring for a few beers or hand out enough cash for more poorly-placed bets. People inquired daily about Mercury's health and attitude. The track maggots hoped he would run forever since they were among the few bettors benefitting from the win streak. Everyone else asked because they wanted to be on the other side when the giant finally fell. Had Mercury been owned by someone else he might have been touted as one of the greatest horses ever. Fortunately for Mercury, he had no idea his pal was so poorly thought of.

Inevitably, people encouraged Willie to run his horse in a stakes race. But knowing the hope was that Mercury would get nervous and run rank, Willie was savvy enough to avoid the temptation, even though the purses were huge. He had a good thing going and was looking to book a race at a notoriously fast track to attempt the world record. Eventually the right horse at the right track became available. Willie had a long hard talk with the woman who'd become their regular jockey about this being an opportunity they couldn't afford to squander.

They had to travel nearly a thousand miles for the race, but things went well, and they arrived without incident. Once Willie had Mercury settled safely in a barn, he bought some beer and tucked into a motel room for a night of TV. The groom had been left behind so the jockey slept in the trailer. Willie knew in his bones that something wonderful was about to happen. Eventually nodding off, he awoke hours later to an infomercial babbling and a warm beer. He crawled into bed and went back to sleep with waving banners and dollar signs littering the pavement of his dreams.

The weather for race day was glorious. The track was sizzling fast all day, and Willie felt sure that when their moment came everything would be conducive to their date with glory. A sense of expectancy hung in the air. The crowd became increasingly aware of it and their energies reached a fever pitch by the time Mercury strutted onto the track amid a cacophonous roar. The other horse was a roan gelding who was a great half-miler that would only quit if pressed extremely hard in deep stretch. Willie wanted the early fractions Splendid Glory could establish, and the horse's owner had previously agreed they would go all out for the world record. The other man knew his horse could lose but felt oddly sympathetic to Willie's desire to see Mercury break the record. Of course, like all the others, he actually expected to win and thusly put his money on the line.

From the gate Mercury seemed to know it was going to be tough. The jockey would state later that she'd never ridden a horse so totally in control of himself. As expected, the first half-mile was torrid. If that was great, the next quarter-mile was fantastic. People would talk well into the night about the other horse slowing in the final eighth-mile and Mercury steadily moving ahead as if on that day he could run forever. After the race it took nearly a full circuit of the track to ease him down. The crowd was delirious when they saw the time of 1:05 and two fifths seconds posted on the tote board. It was a new world record, and they were there to witness it.

Mercury made the national news that day. Every sportscast had some mention of his feat, if only for a few seconds. Some showed footage of the stretch drive, which was an equine work of art. Willie was so flush and happy he bought rounds at the clubhouse bar.

Over strong coffee the next morning, Willie perused the papers, got out his scissors, and collected souvenirs of his and Mercury's triumph. As usual, while the day went on, the media was more interested in the horse than Willie. The wad of money in his pockets proved that once in a great while a cheap hustler could roll one down the pike and score a bullseye. The comfort of that made all disrespect inconsequential.

The problem with guys like Willie is that they lack the internal strength to hold onto success when it finally arrives. Having too much brings out the excessive side of them and starts a decline that rapidly spirals into destitution. It took a while for Willie to screw up, but when he did come off of his roll it was due to a lot of small decisions that turned into big deals. Decisions like staying at parties too late then suffering while he did work that he used to enjoy. Taking care of Mercury was a full-time job, but so was soaking up the glory surrounding a record holder. Willie started farming out too much of the work and the consequences multiplied exponentially. Mercury stayed in shape and kept on winning, but Willie was falling apart day by day.

After a while, Mercury attracted fewer and fewer challengers. Having shown that head to head he was unbeatable, the idea of deposing the king was losing its luster. Willie and Mercury still attracted attention wherever they went, but horse owners became less willing to give their money away. Fortunately, for Mercury's personal pride, Willie never entered him in a race against a group of horses. Seeing him lose was what too many people wanted, and Willie could not and would not grant such satisfaction. Possibly for himself, as much as the horse, Willie's resolve in that area remained firm.

Like many media stars, Mercury hung around in the news for a while, then became another "was somebody once." Replaced by the ever mushrooming explosion of new ideas and talent. He was still a solid performer, but not the main attraction anymore. Willie slowly worked his way back to sitting in front of the TV, watching soaps and caring for his claim to fame. He let the help go when there were no more races to book, but Mercury never missed a day of care. As Willie's original self came back, so did his love for taking care of his horse. He could treasure the fact that he had once been a winner in the giant gamble that is life. Strangely, that had become enough for him. There was money enough to keep them both fed and housed for years to come and dirt to run on when inspired. Loyal friends forever, reminiscing about days of glory and the flash of flying hooves.

Chef

By Mizeta Moon

Scavenger Ed limped away from the dumpster with two zucchinis and a bunch of celery clutched in his grubby hands. Each had bad spots, but to Ed they were just what was needed. Stooping over the battered cardboard box that held his other treasures, he placed them inside. As he did so, his well-worn dirty pants split at the seam. He cursed for a minute, then limped back to the dumpster to see what was available in the Men's Wear department.

Later, new wardrobe procured, but still looking seedy as ever, he limped towards the shelter of the bridge where he would turn over the day's gleanings to Chef. They called him Chef because he'd once been one. One of the greatest, he'd heard said. Worked in a big hotel on the French Riviera, wherever that was, and made dinners fit for kings. All Scavenger Ed knew was that the paunchy old man with gnarled hands could turn half-rotten food into savory stews and life-sustaining heat. They all drank a lot to keep warm, but without grub you died on the sidewalk. Ed had lain in his own piss and puke enough times to know.

Looking at the sky, and gathering clouds made him hobble as fast as his war-wounded leg would allow, considering his burden. His mouth began to water when he thought about what Chef could do with the half a ham he'd found earlier. It seemed so fresh he could scarcely believe someone threw it away. Ed had always been poor, and that state seemed natural to him. He had no hopes, horizons or dreams. He lived right now with a constantly hungry gut. Even though he was one of life's also-rans, whose name was on the program in such fine print no one bothered to read it, these days he was pretty happy. The group under the bridge was doing fairly well with the mix of people huddled in its shelter. It was better than wandering in all directions trying to survive.

It was like having an identity and belonging to a social club. He himself bringing in the food so that Chef could do his part. Each of the others contributing a particular skill or service to the betterment of the group. Take Whitey the Hammer, who used to be a construction boss and built them some decent lean-tos out of old packing crates. Sleeping dry on newspapers was preferable to a cold doorway. Stopping to take a piss on a warehouse wall, he felt the cold breeze signaling rain swooping through previously quiet concrete canyons. He hoped The Kid had gathered lots of wood or the fire would die out early and they'd be forced to sit shivering in cold darkness listening to rain.

Chef sat quietly sharpening his knife, watching Scavenger Ed limp up the small hill it was necessary to climb to get under the bridge. He sighed, then leaned forward to spit the goo from his chew into a rusty can. He told himself for the thousandth time that he needed to leave this place soon for warmer places. Till then, it was nice to have Ed supply them with food. He never knew what he would be cooking, but whatever he was given, he could do something good with it. That was his problem. He was too good. The power and fame he'd gained took their toll in drugs and alcohol consumed to keep pace. In the end, countless hours in kitchens led to a man who was tired and spent. Yet, he could cook for this pack of losers who paid their respect with slurps and clanging utensils and find comfort. There was never a morsel left of anything he prepared. Still watching Ed take forever to climb the hill, he stirred the broth in his single cook pot and threw a few twigs onto the fire beneath it.

His hands hurt him today. The pain had made him scold The Kid several times for not gathering enough wood to last all night. He hated sitting in late night gloom listening to the sounds of a rainy city. It reminded him too much of his war years, when screams of the tortured pierced the black, and gutters ran red with blood. When he was captured by the enemy and forced to cook for them, he'd wanted to poison them, but his lack of courage and

desire to live stopped him from doing so. They'd hurt his hands enough times that
on days such as this he always thought of their sadism and gluttonous consumption while half the world lay starving. He needed his hands to cook, so they hadn't rendered them useless, but still targeted them to punish him when his responses were slow or inadequate.

The two zucchini were in pretty good shape, but the celery would require major surgery. What a beautiful ham, he thought. Smells good. It must have been abandoned by someone who was moving and didn't have time to finish it. Rice. Some barbequed beans so old that he discarded. Then he'd told Ed a thousand times to be selective, but the man had issues, or he wouldn't be living among them. All in all, it was a good haul that also contained three tomatoes and some garlic bread he could use for croutons on the soup. Opening the wooden box that held his spices, he went to work. A slice here. A chop there. Sautee that on an old hubcap. Soon my lads. Soon.

When the meal was well under way, he looked up with a silent message to the Indian they called Firewater whose job it was to procure the wine. An unspoken command produced a quick shuffle and a healthy snort of Thunderbird. He spit into the can and got back to work. No one wanted to make Chef mad before dinner, so anytime he wanted a drink it was there. In the beginning they had fought over alcohol a lot. As a result, dinner was often late or served cold. Chef could be merciless when angered, so if they wanted a hot meal, keeping him happy was the first order of business.

Firewater had always been mean. Kicked out of school, church, and society for his drunken violence. He'd spent so many nights in jail he knew most cops by name. They got where they didn't arrest him unless he hurt someone. He was just another derelict without money to pay fines or retribution, so he was dropped back into the gutter when the city got tired of feeding him. Every day, he managed to find someone who would pay him a few dollars to keep from getting beat up. Those petty extortions kept him drunk and provided his buddies with just enough to keep their whistles wet. On his way back to the bridge, he would stop at the package store where an old Jew sold cheap wine and smokes. He would purchase a few small bottles to pass around and a gallon jug for himself.

Something he didn't know was that lately he had been blacking
out with booze still in the bottle and that his companions pilfered it while he slept. As he snored and wallowed, he kept a good grip on the bottle, so they often had to use straws to siphon it. Firewater never minded giving Chef a drink since he liked to eat and was a lousy cook himself. Prior to joining the group, he often ate cold hot dogs, or any prepackaged meal he could shoplift. When times were especially bad, he would go to a hospitality house and stand in line to sing hymns for watery soup and stale bread.

As he sat waiting for dinner, his florid face revealed a million mileage lines on dirty skin crisscrossed by battle scars and fresh bruises. Waning light made him look like a seedy warrior from some old movie, whose workday was over, who had no need for the night since no glory awaited him. While stars were out on the town, extras like him faded into oblivion.

When each had their bowl of soup and slice of ham, the only sounds were from eating, and there was no conversation. As usual, The Kid tried reaching for seconds before Chef gave the go- ahead and got cuffed away by Whitey the Hammer. Runaway kids were not usually allowed to stay, but this junior outlaw did work around the camp and collected wood for the fire, so they hid him when cops leaned over the rail of the bridge to check them out. Most of the cops were too lazy to traverse the wash and climb the hill to get under the bridge, so they yelled for everyone to stand where they could be seen. The youth was small and easily hidden, so he had been around for quite a while. His parents had beaten him so much he quivered at night and moaned in his sleep. He seemed happy among them, yet no one could imagine what his future held. Before they were through eating, the rain that had been threatening started to fall. Each of them cast a look at the small pile of wood that would not last the night. The Kid looked at no one. He knew where there was a large crate he could break down the next day and gain forgiveness, but for tonight they would be forced to huddle in their lean-tos.

The Kid slept on a pile of rags in Chef's lean-to. That night neither of them slept and lay in the dark listening to rain drip on the roof.

"Chef. Why do people become bums? Are they all runaways like me?"

The old man didn't answer but sat up and spit. He scratched a

bit, sighed, and then lay back down.

"Why are some folks rich and us poor like this? Chef . . . You gotta tell me! You know lots more than I do."

"Losers kid. They're just losers. Not bums. Not men. Not women. Just losers. Each of them born into different circumstances and different parts of a game called life. What you see here and down on the streets are the losers. If a race is run, someone wins and the rest lose. Losers are seldom given the honor of having tried. They are derided, given no portion of the pie and ultimately ignored. Some people are born without limbs or damaged brains and can never compete on equal footing. Others are crippled emotionally by situations they encounter along the way."

"How did you become a loser? Seems to me you have lots of talent and used to be somebody."

Darkness hid the old man's tears. He cried easily now, for he had no shame or self-respect to salvage. The kid had no way of knowing yet how a life could be pulverized by inconsiderate actions and constant friction. How tension builds until you scream or go crazy. How values erode and morals become nonexistent.

"People hurt you kid. They act like they love you, then steal you blind, eat all your food, run up your phone bill, screw your wife, beat your dog, wreck your car. Stuff like that. They swindle each other every day to make money. Always trying to be the one on top. You fall in love and find out that bills and kids can ruin a marriage and result in a broken home like yours. Your father beat you because he had fears and frustrations. He's a loser because his flesh and blood is gone now. People like me with talent get exploited by restaurant owners who work us to death while demanding perfection. Even with all the money and education in the world you can still become an emotional loser."

Talking so much made Chef's mouth dry, so he rose from his resting spot and quietly walked to Firewater's shack. There was about a pint left in the jug, which for once was easily pried from the drunken man's fingers. He drank half of it in one big slug then savored the rest in little mouthfuls while he talked to the kid for hours about the ways of losers.

Near dawn, Chef fell asleep after venting about things he'd kept bottled up for years. The Kid lay there wondering if there was any
reason to live at all. So far things weren't looking too swell. He was still young, however, and the possibility of magic remained. Maybe if he thought good thoughts Scavenger Ed would find a chicken during his day of scrounging. It had been a long time since they'd had chicken.

Hear No Evil

By Mizeta Moon

"I should have bought a new tie," he said to himself as he stood facing the mirror. "This one's seen too many graduations and been laundered more times than I can remember. At least my tuxedo is crisp and freshly laundered. Look at these creases! I could cut myself on them," he said. "What was I thinking? Why didn't I go shopping for such a special occasion?"

His conversation with the image in the mirror remained one-sided. Answering himself might have exposed some form of mental illness. Heaven forbid he plead insanity but admitting that he looked wonderful settled his jangled nerves. Maybe he could get through the night without making a fool of himself. Was he strong enough? Was he ready for the consequences? Would he still know himself in the morning?

Lawrence Fogelthorpe had been headmaster at the Richland School for the Deaf for thirty-seven years. He'd watched thousands of students come and go and was happy to have shared in their gaining skills that would allow them to live productive lives. Most of them were faceless and nameless to him since his administrative duties were all-consuming. But once in a while, particular students captured his attention and became worthy of extra-curricular perusal. Such was the case with Anton Williams and Fredrick Massingale. They were the subject of his most strenuous scrutiny and had completely captured his imagination.

When they came to the school, they were mere boys, barely able to communicate even their most basic needs. However, both were possessed of brilliant minds and rapidly progressed through a curriculum designed to allow students years to grasp knowledge the school imparted. They learned sign language in record time and quickly became capable of signing sentences that were totally comprehensible. Academically, they soared to the head of their class and surpassed every expectation. The fact they would become lovers was not anything Lawrence could have imagined, or even been aware of. He was oblivious to their emotional and hormonal growth, and was merely interested in their classroom achievements, as that was where money came into play. Grants were available for successful programs. Teaching deaf students had paid for his home in Estacada and a cottage in Florence, where he moored his sailboat.

Their love affair first came to his attention when he caught them holding hands in the art museum. He was fascinated by a Monet exhibit on loan from a Chicago gallery and had been quietly communing with water lilies when he'd looked across the room and saw Anton kissing Fredrick next to a Van Gogh. From that point forward, he watched them like a hawk.

After leaving the school, Anton became a successful playwright and Fredrick launched several restaurant ventures that led to wealth and fame. Lawrence felt connected to their glory, as his school had given them the foundation for their success. Without him and his staff, they might have been uncommunicative, forced to live on charity and government programs.

For several years they escaped his monitoring, as other students and school issues vied for his attention. It was only when they made the national news that his interest was rekindled.

Fredrick and Anton had gone on vacation in Mississippi and chartered a fishing boat. Afterwards, they'd booked a table at a five-star restaurant whose claim to fame was converting anyone's catch-of-the-day to succulent fare. When they arrived to claim their seats and consume their meal, they were denied service due to a recent law that had been enacted to allow discrimination based on religious tenets. They were gay and therefore had no right to be served by the bigots who owned the restaurant. Their boisterous disagreement with such treatment resulted in the local police department taking them into custody. While in jail, Anton was beaten by a faggot-hating redneck and nearly died. Fredrick was sentenced to three years in prison for refusing to pay an exorbitant bill for processing the fish they'd submitted. Their handicaps were ignored and the treatment they received was worse than that of a mangy dog.

The ACLU got involved. Protestors surrounded the prison and demanded justice. For months Anton lay unawares in a coma, being treated by staff that was mostly indifferent to his fate, but fearful of reprisal should he die while under their care. Fredrick became a symbol of the unjust treatment of gay people throughout America's southern states. Attorneys volunteered their time to free him and allow the two of them to return to Oregon. When Anton finally recovered, it was a joyful day for thousands of people who'd attended vigils for him. When the ACLU convinced the Mississippi Supreme Court to release Fredrick, game shows and soap operas were interrupted to announce the news. It was a wonderful day in the history of gay mankind. Lawrence Oglethorpe glowed with satisfaction that his wunderkind had prevailed despite seemingly insurmountable odds.

Their return to Oregon and subsequent purchase of a home in Parkrose was newsworthy for several days. Lawrence went to their housewarming party along with several hundred others but withheld his secret from them. He ate canapes, drank champagne and shook a lot of hands while being accredited with providing the impetus fueling their accomplishments. After the soirée, he'd been invited to their wedding that was set for the following month and felt that would be the perfect time to reveal his big surprise. Just the thought of it made him giddy with expectation.

All of that was why he now groomed himself in the mirror and fussed over every detail. When the doorbell rang and announced the arrival of his escort for the evening, he nearly jumped out of his skin. His hands were clammy, and a bead of perspiration had broken out on his forehead. Walking out the door was more like floating on a cloud, and the limo ride to the Unitarian church was surreal. Stepping into a well-lit foyer at the church, he smiled at his companion and beamed at the usher when their invitation was confirmed, and they were led to front-row seats.

The ceremony was magnificent and produced tears of joy in the crowd. The minister used sign language to administer the vows of commitment while a beautiful interpreter spoke aloud. When they placed rings upon each of the others' fingers, Lawrence wept openly.

Afterwards, when the reception line formed, Lawrence stepped forward to give his congratulations to the two men. Grasping each of their outstretched hands simultaneously, he cleared his throat while noting the surprise on their faces.

"I'd like you to meet my fiancé, Gustav," was all Lawrence said, not attempting to suppress his tearful joy.

A Good Credit Score

By Howard Schneider

"**H**ey Willy! Where you going? We need to talk," Dave yelled when he saw Willy ducking behind a clump of rhododendrons next to his ratty little house.

"Aw shit. I don't need this right now. Fucker's gonna hassle me about the money," Willy grumbled, as he stepped out from behind the scraggly growth. "Hey, Dave. What's up, man? I was just checking to see if I need to trim these things."

"What a creep. Pretending he didn't see me. Acting like he cares about those scraggly, half-dead bushes," Dave mumbled as he strode quickly toward Willy, a scowl on his face. "'You got that five hundred?"

"What do you mean five hundred? I only owe you four-fifty. And I'll pay up tomorrow. I got something going. My credit's good," Willy said with as much bluster as he could manage under the circumstances.

"Don't play innocent, Willy boy. You know the terms. It was four-fifty yesterday. Today it's five. Tomorrow it'll be five-fifty. If I was you, I'd find the scratch real fast. You got till midnight. You know where to find me. By the way. Your credit's no good with me or anybody else in this town."

Back in his Mustang, Dave punched a number into his phone. "Yeah?"

"Hey, Max. You around tomorrow morning? I got a collection problem. Might need some muscle."

"No problem. When and where? Who's the target?" Max said without even thinking about it. Max was short on cash and knew Dave would be good for at least fifty, maybe a little more if everything went okay.

"That low-life sleaze-bag Willy Stiletto. If he doesn't pay by midnight, I'll pick you up at ten."

"It'll cost you seventy-five if we're done by noon. A hundred if it's later," Max said.

"Come on Max. This is me, Dave, not an ATM. Fifty's best I can do. All you'd have to do is break a couple fingers. No big deal. We'll be done in ten minutes."

"Alright, if that's all it is. Make it sixty-five and I'm in."

The next morning, Max was thinking about the job with Dave as he poured his second cup of coffee when there was a loud rap at the front door. Max saw Dave's Mustang parked at the curb when he glanced through the living room window. The clock on the wall said it was only eight-thirty.

"That you Dave? You're early," he yelled through the door.

"Yeah, it's me all right. Who'd you think it was, your fairy god mother?" a muffled voice answered. "Open up!"

Max was surprised to see Willy instead of Dave standing on the stoop.

"Willy! What the hell you doing here? What's going on? What you doing with Dave's car? Did he loan it to you? Hey, wait a minute! What's with the gun?"

Max was terrified when Willy pointed a pistol at his gut.

"Whaddya think, Max? You think I didn't know Dave would get you to do his dirty work? That you wouldn't rough me up just cause I don't have his stinking money exactly when he wants it? You think I'm gonna let that happen? And do you think your drugged-out neighbors will pay attention to a gunshot? Dave's not gonna be any help either. I made sure of that," Willy said, staring into Max's eyes.

Before Max could answer, Willy pulled the trigger. The blast propelled the big man back into his house. Willy quickly yanked the door shut and crammed the gun back in his coat pocket. He looked up and down the empty street, then casually walked through the weeds back to the Mustang.

Willy was happy to have paid off his debt. He figured it would improve his credit score.

Dear Diary

By Mizeta Moon

I'd slept in the same alley too long. Gotten complacent. Become comfortable and forgotten the rule of moving on. The night crawlers knew where to find my camp, and while I was away for a moment, they used guile and stealth to steal what little I'd accumulated.

From that time on, I degenerated into utter despondency. Rain was falling copiously, and layers of ice coated the roads consigned to shade. The forecast was for even worse conditions. How badly I missed the coat that had been compressed in my bedroll. Now that I was back on the concrete, my bones ached, and I longed for warmth.

All of this was my fault. For a moment I'd overlooked the fact that one is either predator or prey. I'd chosen to ignore the reality that every organism surrounding me was either beneficial to my survival or a detriment to continuation.

I drifted from corner to corner. Shelter was nearly non-existent. When shared, it was a negotiation that could lead to assault or death in the night. My health failed rapidly, and I became even less of a person than I was when I was merely homeless and destitute. Now I was trapped in the downward spiral of dissolution.

My chance for salvation came from a Susan B. Anthony one-dollar coin I found on the sidewalk. When I first found it, I rubbed its surface in disbelief and wondered how to spend it. To my way of thinking, I had a choice between a cheap snack, and maybe a soda, but somehow found myself asking the Iranian clerk at Seven-Eleven for a scratch-off ticket.

I fully expected it to be another useless stab at the brass ring of success. Picking up a rock from the ground, I scratched off the sectors slowly, relishing the ongoing pain of failure, fully anticipating the misfortune that had been my cloak throughout endless misadventure.

My eyes filled first with disbelief, then wonder, then tears, as I gazed at the numbers. I had won five million dollars. Joy overwhelmed me and I looked at the ticket over and over, still not comprehending that all of this was real. I was numb—anyone could have snatched the ticket from my fingers.

I wish I could tell you that I did good things with the money. That charities became the beneficiaries of my generosity, or that old debts were paid, and favors remembered. Instead, I drank and drugged myself into an even greater state of uselessness. Lying here in detox, with all of it gone and nothing of value to show for it, I should feel shame, but don't. Why, you ask? It was my turn. Didn't I deserve a momentary respite? I know. I know. Such wealth could have transformed my life and gained me long-term comfort. All I can tell you, dear diary, by way of an explanation, is that my fall from grace occurred so long before that event that I no longer had a sense of self-worth. Instead, I was filled with hunger that allowed me to wallow in plentitude.

When released from detox I'll go back to sleeping on the sidewalk and once more be invisible, but for a time bartenders called me by name and dealers greeted me with a smile. The spare change I passed around made me someone on the street. It was a hell of a party while it lasted. Even a few women spent time with me in seedy hotels, smoking crack and drinking. The only regret I have is that the money ran out before my ravaged body died. Now, I'll have to find a new place on streets that grow more crowded with others like me every day.

Motel

By Mizeta Moon

A swarm of insects circled the streetlight and a moth fluttered against my window screen. It had rained earlier, and the air still smelled of it. There was a swishing sound when cars rolled past. Humidity made beads of sweat soak my body. The heat was stifling, but there was nothing I could do except lie in my bed and suffer.

I'd never been to Atlanta before. Never been to any big city for that matter. Born in a sugar cane field, and raised wielding a machete, I knew nothing about the ways of folks outside my little town. We were simple people who baked corn bread and shucked peas while gossiping and sipping a little cane-sugar rum. We helped each other when times were hard and stood knee deep in floods to rescue cats and dogs. We put a few coins in the collection plate while listening to the preacher go on about our sins. Afterward, we'd roast a pig, and half the town would feast.

When the hurricane tore our town to pieces my family had nothing left. We lived on charity for a while, then I started drifting and left the others behind. Had I stayed at home; I wouldn't have been lying in the motel room that night. Even had I starved back home it would have been better than what happened there in Atlanta.

The walls were thin, so I heard them talking while I watched a bat swooping in to devour bugs around the streetlight. They were planning a murder and I could scarcely believe my ears. People died back home, but no one got murdered. Ricky Jenkins robbed the liquor store, but only used a pocketknife and didn't hurt anyone. Mabel Jenkins, his mom, cried when the sheriff took him away, but went right back to work cutting cane so she wouldn't lose her job. I wasn't prepared for life in a place where danger lurked in dark corners and even darker hearts.

Like a fool, I stuck my ear to the wall and listened more closely. My breathing got so loud they heard and banged on the wall. Told me to mind my own business or else. I tried. Oh, how I tried to ignore them, but the window was open, and sounds carried on the night air.

They must have decided I'd heard too much and had to be eliminated. They had no idea I'd never seen their faces and knew no names. Had they walked away in the morning and carried out their plan, I wouldn't have been much help to the police. I'd already thought about calling the police several times but didn't have a dime for the phone. I'd spent my last four dollars for the room and was nearly out of gas. Had no hopes of work, so getting involved wouldn't have been very smart. I was unprepared when two men burst into the room and began to pummel me.

I'd wrestled with other boys. I had some rough-and-tumble moments in my day, but never a fist fight. My skill at defending myself was untested. Though I was strong from my time in the cane fields, they were larger and heavier and skilled with their fists. I was taking a beating and needed help, or I might die.

I regret what happened, but due to that experience I am now warier when traveling. I still have the machete and keep it sharpened. One never knows when they might stare danger in the face. When my hand found it under the bed and grasped its well-worn handle, I felt relieved. Heaving mightily, I dislodged the one who was holding me down while the other kicked me. Once on my feet, I swung and kept doing so till the room ran with gore. Afterwards, I gathered my meager belongings and fled.

The man on the radio said they were very bad men. That most likely other gangsters had executed them. No one ever came looking for me, even though I signed my name in the book. I guess the coppers were happy to have them gone and willing to leave it be. Since then, I've picked a lot of cotton, then spent the money in juke joints. Done a hundred jobs and stuck with none. The thing is . . . I've seen more of the country, all the while working hard not to remember that night in Atlanta. But I do keep looking over my shoulder just in case somebody comes.

Now Where Is She?

By Howard Schneider

Barney Klagger rushed room to room looking for his wife, Hilda. She was nowhere to be found.

"God damn it, Hilda! Where are you?" Barney's frustration was building. "There's someone here wants to see you. She's in the front room."

He went down to the basement and searched everywhere—the remodeled rec room, the laundry room, the furnace room, even the pantry where Hilda stored all the canned vegetables and fruit she put up each year, some of the jars going back decades.

No Hilda.

"Maybe she went out to the back yard, "he mumbled on his way back up the stairs. "Or maybe up to her sewing room. I'll check that first. Damn that woman."

In the hallway he opened the door to the stairwell that went upstairs, but instead encountered coats and raingear arranged neatly on a row of hangers, and an assortment of boots and other shoes on the floor. He slammed the door shut and shifted over to the one next to it. He opened that one, stood staring at the stairs for a second, then started climbing.

"You up here?" he cried when he reached the landing.

Again, no Hilda.

Back downstairs, he went through the kitchen and out onto the rear porch.

"Damn that woman!" he repeated. He stood on the porch steps and scanned the yard, seeing the turned-under garden, the row of azaleas along the cedar fence, the freshly-painted side of the garage.

But no Hilda.

"Hilda?" He yelled.

No reply.

He went inside and made his way to the living room.

"She must have gone out front," he said to himself.

He glanced at the woman sitting on the sofa flipping through a magazine, then opened and stepped through the doorway Standing on the stoop, he looked around their little patch of grass, then up and down the street.

"Hilda?"

No answer.

He went back inside.

"Damn that woman!"

The woman on the sofa looked up, then laid the magazine aside. She reached for a tiny device laying on the coffee table in front of her. She inserted it into her ear, then said, "Barney! What are you doing?"

"Who are you?" Barney answered, a puzzled look on his unshaven face.

"Barney, Honey. It's me, your wife. Hilda."

Barney didn't say anything, just stood there looking at her.

Hilda picked up the magazine off the sofa cushion and laid it on the table, then rose to her feet and went over to where Barney stood at the still-open door.

"How about a cup of tea. We'll make your favorite kind." She shut the door, then took Barney's trembling hand firmly in hers and led him to the kitchen.

Obsession

By Linda Burk

As I sit here stirring the peanut oil into my jar of natural, crunchy, non-homogenized peanut butter, I can only imagine the number of jars of peanut butter I have consumed in my lifetime. Sandwiches on squishy-soft, white bread for school lunches, snacks, and summer camp. It's what I want when I return from vacation after eating too many rich foods at restaurants. Of course, I try to make it healthier now and have ditched the white bread. These days I favor the whole grain, high-fiber kind I scorned as a child.

I come by this obsession honestly. My Dad loved to eat a big scoop of peanut butter whenever he was hungry, and his favorite evening snack was grilled peanut butter and Miracle Whip salad dressing sandwiches. The rest of the family turned up our collective noses and preferred grilled cheese. Of course, we insisted on Velveeta. It's not hard to see how those extra calories landed on us and stuck fast.

No one really knows the complete history of peanut butter. Peanuts were known as early as 950 BC and originated in South America. By the 1800's, the first commercial crop was grown in Virginia. It is said that Dr. John Harvey Kellogg patented a process for creating peanut butter from raw peanuts. He served it to his toothless patients in the Kellogg Sanitarium. I learned this and many other facts about Dr. John Harvey Kellogg from the book "The Nuts Among the Berries."

In 1903, Dr. Ambrose Straub patented a peanut butter-making

machine. As time went on, commercially available peanut butter was made from roasted peanuts (which I believe made for a much tastier product).

You can ask any number of folks what their favorite addition to the peanut butter sandwich is. I bet that's a good conversation starter. The list would be endless: butter, jelly, honey, Nutella, bananas, pickles, mustard, bacon, raisins, mayonnaise, or goat cheese, not to mention all the cakes, cookies, pies, candy, entrees, and (of course) ice cream that includes peanut butter. What's your favorite?

I must admit, it's only one of the foods I could call an obsession, but our lives would be pretty boring without it.

Trailer Trash

By Mizeta Moon

I'd been downsized without warning. Was given a pink slip and a severance check in the same envelope and was expected to be grateful. Ordered to clean out my desk and vacate the premises immediately, or the severance would be rescinded. Some lawyer at the corporate office was earning his pay by building unbreachable walls around me. What could I do but comply? I'd seen others protest and be carried out by police, jailed, or left bloody on the sidewalk. Having no desire to follow suit, I maintained my dignity and walked out quietly while my co-workers shook their heads and looked away, grateful it wasn't them.

Within a year I was on the ropes. House gone. Girlfriend, too. Unemployable because of a memo in my personnel file from a non-existent vice president accusing me of stealing company funds. I hadn't but couldn't prove it after the computer dumped the story onto social media and I had my fifteen minutes of infamy. Truth was, others were milking the company cow and wanted me out of the way. Why my future had to be compromised by a lie was a mystery that led me to wonder what I'd done or who I'd crossed to deserve such a fate. But that didn't matter. The important thing was using my last five thousand dollars to find a way to survive. I was only forty and so far away from Social Security that predictions of its failure might deny my ever reaping a benefit.

I'd taken the Number 72 bus to Clackamas Town Center just for something to do. Spending was out of the question unless it was for food or vital necessities. My room in a weekly motel was costing a fortune I didn't have. I needed time to think, so I wandered the mall acting like someone who could make a purchase if a window displayed something irresistible. Getting low on energy, I splurged for a Cinnabon and a cup of coffee with a free refill and sat down in a comfy chair to watch humanity stroll by. After savoring my treats, I chastised myself for such wanton indulgence. I'd seen too many beggars on the freeway ramps and didn't want to be one of them. Such license was the slippery slope to penury.

Leaving the air conditioned shopping plaza behind, I decided to walk awhile. After crossing 82nd Avenue, I took random lefts and rights, generally aiming towards downtown. I roamed streets I'd never traveled by car, let alone knew existed. It was my first true experience of Southeast Portland in its mixed bag of glory. Some homes were freshly painted, and flowers were well-tended. Others glared with too many cars out front that obviously hadn't moved for some time. Roses bloomed heartily or scratched towards the sky with shriveled limbs. Pansies and geraniums proliferated in window boxes or struggled to survive in yards filled with broken bikes and shabby lawn furniture. Surly underfed dogs guarded patches of dirt where nothing grew. Blaring music issued from corner bars and the sweet sounds of birds filled a neighborhood park. My senses reeled as I took in other people's lives and pondered my own.

I'd made it to Powell and thought about turning north to Division when I saw the girl of my dreams. A downtrodden Airstream trailer with a crinkled FOR SALE sign in its window stole my heart. I was smitten immediately and there was no turning back. She was crying out for love and I was in need of shelter. From the moment I touched her skin I knew we belonged together. Backed against the curb as she was, I could only think of shielding her from further harm. Turning back the tides of entropy and atrophy, filling her with new life.

The guy wanted twenty-five hundred. A couple days into negotiations I waved fifteen cash in his face and he signed over the title. I could tell he was just like me. Circling the drain and desperate to stay afloat. Capitalism is based on opportunists exploiting the vulnerable, and for once I was in the driver's seat.

My truck hadn't been driven in some time but had half a tank of gas and air in the tires. No insurance, since I'd let that lapse, but it fired up right away and purred in anticipation, as if it knew what was in store. It took me a while to get the hookup right and the turn signals plugged in, but I was proud as hell when I rolled away with my new home. I had to give the motel owner an extra twenty bucks a week to park it in a gravel lot alongside the cottages, but felt it was a toll to be paid on the way to a new life, although that was about to change as well. Running low on cash, I had to give up the motel within a few weeks and face the uncertainty that had loomed on the horizon for quite some time.

At first, I moved to some pretty sketchy places. Paid by the week while I assessed needed repairs and the overall condition of my new home. Between trailer parks, I overnighted on many of Portland's quiet streets, but always moved on in the morning out of respect for those who paid taxes and still had a job. One afternoon I was buying five bucks worth of gas at a mini-mart and ogling over-cooked hot dogs rolling on a stainless steel treadmill when a man wearing overalls and work boots tapped me on the shoulder. When I turned to face him, my destiny changed again.

"That's your Airstream ain't it?" he asked excitedly. "She's a real beaut. What'd ya give for her?"

Should I resent his nosiness? Dump on him for being friendly? Ask why he needed to know? No. I decided to be polite and I've never regretted that decision.

"More than I could afford, but I wanted her. Know what I mean? You like trailers?" I asked.

"Hell. I'm a trailer fanatic," he replied. "Fix em up and sell em all over the world. Buy that one if you've a mind to sell her."

"Naw. I'm good . . . but you can see her if you like."

We became best friends. He helped me restore my trailer to good as new using salvaged parts, and when I couldn't afford something that had to be purchased, he let me sweep up around his shop or do something he could pay me for. Everything functions just fine now, and I'm often parked under a tree on a remote corner of his property. When he finally got around to asking about my past, our relationship shifted to a new level. These days I work in his front office, manage his internet home page and do the books, like I did where I worked before. Only now, I can do it from anywhere with my laptop, mobile phone and Wi-Fi connection. Call me trailer trash and I don't care. I can move away from hardship, conflict, and sorrow. Most people are stuck with their neighbors and whatever grief they leave on their doorstep. If my neighborhood takes a nosedive, I can unplug, roll down the road, and stick my cord into another socket. New scene, different people. A whole new vibe.

The few square feet I have to call my own often finds itself in a meadow surrounded by butterflies and hummingbirds. I've parked at the beach and pondered the majesty of waves. Wandered through trees older than I and seen the sunrise sparkle across morning dew. Been touched by vapors transcending into essences on the way to the next thing, which is just around the bend.

Pain

By Mizeta Moon

It was supposed to be an amazing excursion. Wild beasts lunging at the Land Rover while we snapped photos to share on Facebook. Camping under the stars on the African plains in tents designed to keep out bugs and rain. Natives shaking rattles, clanging bells, banging drums and raising clouds of dust with their stamping feet. Eating exotic foods prepared by chanting women in wrap-around dresses and headscarves. The usual roll-out for tourists willing to spend a few bucks being entertained by things outside their normal experience. The providers had rehearsed and carried out the scenario so many times they had to feign excitement and conceal their boredom while waiting for the financial payoff. Quite often things don't turn out as planned, but the consequences are not always as dire as when the wheels completely come off and everything runs amok.

I'm sorry, but I can't tell you what country it was. Geography is not my long suit, and my memory is filled with horrible deeds these days, so details escape me.

I'd shopped L.L. Bean for great safari shorts and everything one would need in a foreign land. I had bottled water, extra tampons and underwear, lots of toothpaste and my favorite book of poetry for those quiet moments alone. There were seven of us in all and I only knew two of them casually. The rest were wanderers like me. Booking cruises, seeing the world. Spending what they'd earned on enriching their souls.

Things started out OK. We saw some great scenery, ate everything in sight and listened to the sounds of a nocturnal symphony every night. Everything seemed fine until the fifth day.

We woke to sounds of gunfire. Echoing distantly to be sure but threatening all the same. Feeling uneasy, I asked about it.

"Rebel forces," someone answered.

What did that mean? Had we stumbled into a local conflict? Was there a war on? What was happening? And why was no one forthcoming with reassurances? We depended on our guides for safety and they seemed indifferent to our fate, but truly concerned for their own. I watched them closely and somehow knew we were in trouble.

I would describe them to you, but why? Would it make them lesser or greater monsters? Whether they were tall or small, fat, muscled or slim would not change how badly they defiled me. They were men looking for receptacles to house their violence, lust, and desire for supremacy. Who was I to believe I could repel their advance? Begging for mercy fell on deaf ears and the cruelty they bestowed was something no civilized person could ever imagine or comprehend.

They stopped us on the rutted dirt track we were traversing after breaking camp. An armored personnel carrier bristling with machine guns greeted us around a bend shielded by foliage that had made me marvel at life's diversity. My perusal of its beauty was shattered by the squealing of brakes and the curses of our guides, who would be the first ones shot and left bleeding by the road.

They came to me and used me for hours upon hours. After dragging me into a filthy hovel they would sweat over me time after time while my body cried out in agony for rest and sustenance that only came with the occasional drink of water. Battered and bruised, I lay in my despicable trappings and pled for the death of my captors and myself. Unwashed, unfed, I became uncaring about anything but escape. Surviving horrors of the moment by dreaming of what I used to be. Relishing scraps of food thrown onto the floor of my cage when they finally appeared.

In the movies or on TV, the hero shows up in the nick of time to rescue the fair maiden from harm. Books drag you to the very last page to kill the bad guy and have the central characters kiss their way into blazing sunsets. It wasn't like that. It was suffering added to misery and pain. After an immeasurable time passed, things changed, but not due to outside intervention

I was dragged across concrete, then dirt and gravel. They'd tired of me, and it was as simple as that. They found no more pleasure in penetrating me and thus consigned me to the trash. Into the back of a truck I went. I endured a bumpy ride on unyielding steel floorboards, only to be dumped in a heap outside the U.S. Embassy. Broken pelvis, ruptured kidney, damaged cornea and multiple lacerations. A plethora of injuries to the body, but unforgiveable damage to the soul. Why I wasn't murdered and interred in a shallow grave remains a mystery. The only thing I can come up with is that they wanted the terror to haunt my mind for the rest of my days.

Can you understand why I'm bitter? Have you felt such pain? Been brutalized to the point of insanity? How many others have suffered similar fates? How often throughout time and in every moment?

I understand that my torment was not unique. I know many others have died at the hands of heartless captors. At least I have a room in a house by the lake and the doctors say I'm going to get better. I doubt it somehow, for I have been ravaged. Covered by true evil and left for dead. Pain is more than a broken body. It is a spirit shattered by the wantonness of man.

Grandkids

By Howard Schneider

When my two grandsons walk through the front door, they immediately take possession of the sofa and sit as far away as possible from where I'm comfortably ensconced in my big brown Lazy Boy recliner. Without hesitation, apology, or embarrassment, they fire up the little black devices they hold so lovingly in their small hands, as if they were precious treasures. In a flash they're immersed in whatever world they've clicked and tapped their way into. From then on, the only part of them I see is the tops of their heads.

I frequently babysit them when my daughter and her husband go out to some restaurant, or perhaps to a party or concert. But, as it turns out, I really don't have to do all that much. Not like when they were smaller. It seems not that long ago we enjoyed board games or walked to the park where they played on the swings and monkey bars. We even went to the occasional movie or to the ice-cream shop down the block. No more, though. Now it's just their device stuff. Sometimes I can't even get them to eat the pizza I order in.

Not wanting to give up on the relationship, I try to lure them out of their electronic trances by offering to tell them about what I did for fun when I was their age, or about some family secret. But as soon as I say, I remember when . . . and start to recount an exciting childhood adventure, they give me a look that says I'm the most irrelevant object in the room, then return to whatever it is they're consumed by.

Today when I tried to engage their attention, the older of the two, ten-year-old Gregory, as if out of kindness, said, "That's okay, Grandpa. You don't have to entertain us. We're into a really cool game with a guy in New York and his cousin in Atlanta. It's over the net. They're winning, but me and Jimmy are catching up. Why don't you watch football or something? It won't bother us."

It saddens me that they don't care about me or what I once was, or what lessons and insights I might contribute to their lives. On the other hand, maybe that's just what progress is all about, discarding the past, embracing the new, and following the path forward. After all, is my generation's legacy so wonderful that it should be adopted by the next? Don't they have the right to forge their own future?

Maybe I need to back off. Leave the kids alone. To their own devices, so to speak. Accept that I'm no longer of interest. At least not to this generation. Outdated, expired. Maybe I should just be happy to be alive and still be capable of being enthralled by the endless stream of sports that floods my big screen through the not-inexpensive generosity of cable channels.

So, what if I don't care about those little self-engrossed dwarfs? If they don't care about me, why should I give a damn about them? Tit for tat, as the saying goes.

But wait a minute, I say to myself. Is this really the way I want my family to evolve? Or, perhaps, degenerate?

No! There's got to be a better alternative. Something other than giving way to an intractable separation of generations. Maybe us old guys can learn from them, even if it's not a two-way street. Hmm, maybe I'll give it a try.

"Hey guys, whose side can I be on?" I boldly interrupt as I take the smart phone my daughter left with me earlier in the evening out of my pocket and turn it on. "Is there a password for the game? How about I be on the New York kid's side?"

"Okay, grandpa. You can be Black Wolf," Gregory said, glancing up briefly from the little screen glowing brightly in front of him and lighting up his face. "But you gotta be really mean, Black Wolf's one of the bad guys."

Hunger

By Mizeta Moon

Tears flowing down my face turn into rivers of mud. I could cry forever and not wash away the plague that has shriveled my core and turned me into a well of sorrow. My coating of dust is worn like a shroud that can never be removed, for as one layer washes away another soon takes its place. Dark clouds hover on every horizon and what was green is now withered and sere. Once there was bounty, and abundance filled every valley, lane, and pasture. What rain comes now brings no crops to fill tables of those left behind. Those who couldn't flee were sentenced to hunger.

They called us Sooners. We cheated to get the land and now some folks are saying that endless dust is our punishment. Preachers say we've sinned, but how can I have harmed anyone at the age of ten? I wasn't even alive when my grandpa drove a team of mules and a milk cow across the prairie in search of a homestead. My pa never liked farming or working from dawn to dusk. He drank away his inheritance and let the land go fallow. Ma was the one who provided, by raising chickens and taking in sewing to barter for flour and lard. When Pa died and left us alone, my ma and me were not prepared for winds that swept everything away. For dust that choked our cow and sent her underfed carcass to the ground. For people leaving in wagons or on horseback and in autos laden with their worldly goods. We sold our half-starved mules for a rasher of bacon, some corn meal, and a dozen eggs. That was a month ago, and since then Ma gets skinnier by the day. I know she's sick and I can't leave her. Even if I started walking, I wouldn't know where to   go.

My belly hurts and I dream of food when I fall into restless sleep. Even my juice harp sounds sad when I muster enough saliva to play it. It used to spark a lively jig after a dinner of chicken, biscuits, and gravy. It's all I have left to sell, but nobody wants it. Even the house is stripped bare except for Ma's bed. If we had food there's no pot for cooking. I ate a bug yesterday and might try worms tomorrow if rain brings them out of hiding. Between the dust that never quits blowing and the howls of coyotes ravaging the corpses of those lain down, there should be a path for escape or a moment of silence. I must find them soon or become another specter haunting the porch of a house where hunger remains the only resident.

Shoofly Pie

By Linda Burk

An old song popularized by Dinah Shore in 1946 goes, Shoofly pie and apple pandowdy make your eyes light up and your tummy say howdy. I'm not sure what apple pan dowdy is, but I know shoofly pie is a lip-smacking-good treat.

It doesn't look very appetizing with its brown filling and a few crumbs on top. Most people on the west coast have no idea what it is. But if you take a trip to Lancaster County, Pennsylvania you can ask the Pennsylvania Dutch. This group originated when William Penn settled Pennsylvania as a holy experiment for religious tolerance. German and Swedish Christian Anabaptist Mennonites and Amish flocked to the Lancaster area. They came to America by ship, bringing only a few food staples, such as flour, lard, molasses, brown sugar, salt, and spices. Enterprising women making do invented shoofly pie out of the simple ingredients they had on hand. Baking was done in large outdoor ovens. When the pies were cooling, a bit of the molasses pooled on the top and attracted flies. Thus, the name shoofly pie.

The pies are a simple mix of molasses, hot water, and baking soda. When combined, the ingredients foam like a volcano. This is quickly poured over a layer of crumbs in a pie shell and baked, resulting in a wet-bottom shoofly pie.

When we lived in West Virginia, we had the chance to help make sorghum syrup, which I used to make delicious shoofly pies. Sorghum cane is a source of sugar that was brought from Africa in the 17th century. Farmers harvest it in early autumn. A tractor is attached to a press which is driven in a wide circle. I could imagine using donkeys 100 years ago for the process. Green liquid from the cane stalks flows into troughs which have wood fires burning beneath each section. As the liquid moves along the trough it changes to a deep brown colored syrup. Of course, it attracted bees and flies, so we continually shooed them away.

When our oldest son requests this pie for his birthday each year, we devour it quickly so there's no need to shoo flies away.

Nightmare at the County Fair

By Linda Burk

County Fairs are a big thing in Pennsylvania. Folks gather to see the spiffed-up farm animals, chickens and rabbits of every color and size, old fashion farm equipment, and the 4-H display of art, sewing projects, canned goods, and delicious-looking cakes and pies. Blue ribbons were sprinkled throughout the display hall indicating the best of show.

When my coworker asked me to be a baked goods judge at a small county fair, I jumped at the chance. I thought of all those delectable pies and elegant-looking cakes. With some difficulty I found the small county fairgrounds on the appointed day. It was a miniature version of the country fair that I had attended. They had a fenced-in arena for the pigs and sheep, stalls for the horses, and cages of chickens pecking at hapless bugs who landed in their cages. And of course, the food carts, with the aroma of frying funnel cakes, inviting all to reach for their wallets regardless the time of day.

I found the baked goods judging area and received my assignment. I was to judge the kid's baked goods. I stopped in my tracks, wide-eyed and mouth open, when I saw the six-foot table loaded with cupcakes. There must have been 40 cupcakes of all colors and descriptions: chocolate with white icing, white with chocolate icing, icing with sprinkles, a few with blue or pink icing, and several with cherries. It seemed like every kid in the county had entered the contest. My job was to judge each cupcake on appearance, texture, and taste. Appearance was a snap, but texture and taste was more difficult. I had to take a bite of each of the forty cupcakes! They gave me a bottle of water and a knife. After tasting

112

four or five cupcakes, my taste buds went numb. The cloying sweetness was overwhelming! And I still had thirty-five more cupcakes to go! Some of the little girls were standing by the table, eyes wide as I tasted their special cupcake. It was cupcake hell! I'm sure it was punishment for my love of sweets all these years.

I slowly made my way through the remaining entries, randomly placing blue and red ribbons on the nearest entries. My stomach was churning, my head aching, and I had enough heartburn to last a lifetime. I swore off cupcakes forever. It was months before I could touch anything sweet. I still shudder when I walk pass Saint Cupcake. Those little cakes may look inviting, but I know what's lurking with that first bite.

Off the Grid

By Howard Schneider

"Come on, Tony. Don't be stupid," she would plead, closer to panic every time the subject came up. Angie, four years older, had been a mother figure to her brother, Tony, since their parents were killed in an auto accident six years earlier. The loss of his father, who he loved with absolute devotion, devastated the sixth-grader, and he never got back on track. No drive. No focus. Getting through each day was all he could manage.

"It's not stupid, Angie. Pot's gonna be legal soon. There's no risk. All I have to do is sell good weed cheaper than the legal marijuana shops do. No big deal."

But his optimistic claims failed to convince Angie. "The cops, or DEA, or somebody, will discover what you're doing. They're watching and listening to all of us. Or a competitor, or maybe an upset customer; somebody's gonna want to do you in for some reason or other, or maybe steal your stuff," she argued.

"I won't get caught. Nobody's gonna hassle me. I'm gonna live off the grid—no trace of me. It'll be like I don't even exist. Cash only. No bank. Untraceable disposable mobile phones. No records. No nothing. Just pot and money," Tony responded defiantly.

His mind was made up and she wasn't going to change it.

Within two years, Tony was moving eight to twelve pounds a month, depending on the yield of his home-grown. He had three kinds of customers. The first category, the one with the most potential for growth, consisted of the legal shops he supplied off the books. It had to be good enough to compete with the super-hybrids they carried. So far, the re-tooled Guatemalan he'd developed had no problem in that regard. Since he couldn't grow enough himself to meet the demand, he also bought from a Mexican cartel guy he knew only as Poncho. He got six pounds on the first of every month when they met in the parking lot of the Costco in Northeast Portland. It was a high-test Sensimilla hybrid, definitely the real thing and justified upper-end pricing.

As for his second customer, every two weeks a motorcycle gang bought two pounds of the Mexican and a pound of his home-grown. He delivered it to a huge, long-haired, tattooed guy named Crank; they met in Gresham at Billy's Bar and Grill at 10 p.m. on the first and 15th of every month. This guy was big-time scary, as if close to erupting any minute. Tony went to great extremes not to upset him; always showed up on time, thanked him for the business, didn't bother to count the money he was paid, just stuffed it in his pocket, and promised to see him in two weeks.

The third-level customer was his connection to local street guys that sold mostly dime bags to kids and yuppies. That bunch was handled through a guy named Little Fatty. He took whatever was left after Tony's other sales.

As far as Tony was concerned, nothing could go wrong. Why? Because he was living off the grid. The house he shared was in his buddy's name. He drove an unregistered car. No utility listings, cell phone account or insurance policies. He even had a phony driver's license: his photo but a different name; James Hanson. As far as official Portland was concerned, he didn't exist.

But then, one fateful day, he made an exception to his rule. Maybe it was over-confidence, or just stupidity, it makes no difference now. In response to an irresistible TV commercial, he threw caution to the wind and applied for a BankAmerica credit card. He even used his real name.

When the envelope arrived at Angie's apartment a few weeks later, she held on to it until Tony came over for their once-a-month dinner together. Angie knew it would be him when her buzzer buzzed at 7 sharp.

"Hey, Sis. How's things?" he said, a big smile on his face as he handed her a bouquet of her favorite flowers, yellow roses.

In spite of the complete separation of their worlds, they still maintained the strong closeness created by their parent's death. Over one of her delicious Italian dishes and a good wine, they talked about old times and memories, TV series they both watched, and about Angie's blossoming career and recent promotion to vice president at the commercial real estate firm where she worked. But they never talked about Tony's so-called business.

As far as Tony was concerned, off the grid meant that Angie know nothing about what he did: not where he lived, or what he drove; no visible relationship what-so-ever. Although Tony didn't think there was any danger in what he did, he still didn't want her connected to him in any way, just in case. A guy could never be too careful, especially when it came to a sister he loved and would protect at any cost.

As Tony was preparing to leave. Angie remembered the Bank of America envelope and gave it to him.

"Oh, yeah," he said, feeling the shape of the card inside. "It's probably the credit card I applied for. Hope you don't mind me using your address," he said sheepishly. "You know, staying off the grid, right?"

Angie wasn't thrilled about the address thing, but didn't object since there was nothing she could do about it at that point. *What harm could come of it, anyway?* she thought to herself.

He bid her good night and best wishes for the vacation she was leaving for the following morning. A much-needed one-week break in a remote part of Costa Rica.

"Not even cell phone connection," she yelled at him happily as he walked down her sidewalk and to his car parked two streets away.

Tony's troubles began the next day. The morning started out okay, like always. No sign of anything unusual. He met Poncho at noon for his monthly delivery. Poncho counted the payment while Tony checked the merchandise. Everything was in order.

His next meet was with Little Fatty midafternoon. He stashed his backpack containing the six pounds from Poncho and the bag he had prepared for Fatty in the wheel well in the trunk, repositioned the rubber floor mat, and headed to a bar on Sandy

Boulevard where he always had lunch when he was in that part of town.

He parked in a secluded lot behind the bar and entered through the rear door, passed through the kitchen and into the bar, just like always.

"Hey, Tony. How's it going?" the bartender called out as he entered and took a stool. "The usual?"

"Hey, Maria. Yeah. Burger and a beer."

Tony had known Maria for two years and trusted her completely. If her brusque personality and outrageous tattoos didn't turn off most people, although her rumored connections to one of Portland's most notorious Mexican drug gangs might. But she never hassled Tony. Never mentioned his business, even though she probably knew what he was into. Tony had no worries about her.

"Gotta go, Maria," he said an hour later, laying down a twenty and not waiting for change.

"Thanks, Tony. See you next time, "she said, watching him leave through the door into the kitchen. Checking his watch, he saw that he had just enough time to get to the strip mall in southeast Portland where Fatty would be waiting. Perfect timing. After that, he could go home and tend his plants before his delivery to Crank that night. Everything was looking good. He felt great.

As Tony approached his car, he noticed the broken driver-side window and that the trunk lid was ajar.

"What the hell? Oh, no!" he cried. He knew the dope would be gone. And it was. That's when the worst nightmare Tony could ever have imagined started.

Not only was the pot gone, so was everything else; his disposable, pre-pay phone, the pistol he kept under the seat, even his designer sunglasses, high-power flashlight, and Buck hunting knife.

He was overcome with panic. The loss of his stash was a major disaster, the worst part being the promised delivery to the motorcycle gang. He had enough home-grown, but if he didn't have the Mexican. Crank was gonna be real cranky. The only thing he could do was get another four pounds from Poncho, enough for that night and two weeks later. But he had no phone. Even if he could reach Poncho, he might not have enough for a short-notice sale. "I've got to get a phone fast and call him," Tony mumbled to himself. "Those motorcycle maniacs aren't gonna like it if I don't show up."

If Poncho had what he needed, Tony just had to come up with $6000. He had $4500 in his emergency reserve at the house. He'd have to borrow the rest from his roommate, Zack.

Twenty minutes later Tony had a new disposable phone and caught Zack at home. "I need to borrow $1500, man. I been robbed and have to make another buy so I can do a delivery tonight. I can pay you back after that."

"Sorry, buddy, no can do. Just made a buy myself. Took just about everything I had. I could give you $400. Will that help?" Zack told him.

Tony said, "Not enough, but I'll take it. Still $1100 short."

"Maybe your guy will let that much ride till tomorrow," Zack offered.

"Yeah, maybe. I'll see what he says."

Luckily, Tony was able to reach Poncho. He had plenty of stock and could supply another four pounds. But when Tony said, Poncho, mi amigo, I can give you $4900 now but I'll have to pay the $1100 tomorrow. I ran into some bad luck and need a day's worth of credit.

Poncho responded immediately, a hint of irritation in his voice, "I don't do credit, *amigo*. Call if you come up with the bucks. But before 8 o'clock. I'll be out of reach after then." After a brief pause, Poncho continued, this time in a far from friendly voice. "One more thing, Mr. Tony. Don't make a habit of calling me. You know I don't do business this way. Stick to our schedule. And ditch that phone. Get another one if you call again."

Tony knew not to argue, especially not to beg, a sure sign of weakness. As soon as he clicked off, he removed the chip from the phone and crushed it under his heel, then threw the phone in a trash can. That's when he remembered his newly acquired credit card. It had a limit of $3000. He'd collect $5500 from the motorcycle guy and pay off the card the next day, then get back on track with his business. He checked the time; 4:20. Plenty of time to get to the bank and draw an advance. He relaxed. Everything was gonna be okay. A Bank of America branch was only 15 minutes away.

At 4:35 Tony got in line behind four people at the only open teller's window. When it was his turn, he handed his card to the teller and said, "I'd like a $1100 advance. "He tried hard not to reveal his slight anxiety. This was his first time in a bank in several years.

"Yes sir, it'll just take a minute," the teller said in a friendly manner. But when he swiped the card through the card reader, a frown appeared on his face. "Sorry, sir. This card hasn't been activated yet. You'll have to do that before this transaction can be completed. I'll need to see your ID, as well."

Ignoring the teller's request for ID, Tony said, "How do I do that?" a hint of panic in his voice.

"Easy. Call the number on back of the card, then you can do it automatically," the teller explained.

"Can I borrow your phone? I'll do it now."

"Sorry. There's no phones at these windows. Ask one of the officers at the lobby desks. They'll be happy to help you."

Tony checked his watch as he walked towards the only one of three desks that was occupied; the time was 4:50.

The plaque on the desk said Vice President Customer Services. The suited man was talking on the phone while a customer sat in the chair across from him, leafing through a stack of documents. Tony edged up to the desk, an anxious look on his face.

"I'll be with you as soon as I finish with this customer," the VP said, interrupting his phone conversation for a second. The customer gave Tony a dirty look, then turned back to his papers.

Ten minutes flew by without a break in the man's phone conversation. Precisely at five o'clock, a uniformed security guard entered the lobby and announced that the bank was closing, and everyone had to leave.

"I need to use the phone and get an advance," Tony cried out toward the guard.

"Sorry, sir. You'll have to come back tomorrow. We open at nine."

"But I need it now!" Tony said, much too loudly for a bank lobby.

"Sir! You'll have to leave now!" the guard said in no uncertain tone.

Reluctantly, Tony left without further comment, the security guard close behind him.

"Try the ATM, "the guard yelled as Tony walked across the parking lot towards his car.

"Yeah, thanks," Tony replied, glancing at the ATM on the side of the bank building.

"I gotta get another phone and activate this damn card. Then I can use that ATM thing," Tony mumbled.

Twenty minutes later, Tony had another burner and successfully activated the card. Like the teller said, it was easy. But he cringed at the thought that he had taken another step that drew him further into the all-encompassing grid.

With the card in hand, he rushed back to the bank's ATM. This would be another first in his journey into a new world. A little intimidated by the process, he slipped his card into the slot, then read the words that suddenly appeared on the little screen.

Enter your passcode now.

"What the. . ." he said out loud, totally perplexed by this command. "What the hell is a passcode?"

Just as he was about to smash his fist into the screen in total frustration, an elderly man walked up behind him as if he were going to wait for his turn to use the machine.

Tony turned to him and said, "What's a passcode?"

The man was surprised at the question and at first thought it might be a joke. But due to Tony's panicky demeanor, he quickly said, "It's the code to access your account so the computer knows it's really you and not somebody trying to rip you off."

"How can I get one of those codes?" Tony asked, even more agitated.

"You create it when you set up an account with the bank, "the man replied.

Tony's panic rose another notch. There was no way for him to do that with the bank closed.

"How can I get my card back?" he screamed at the man, as if his predicament was the stranger's fault.

The man stepped forward and instructed Tony how to terminate his attempted transaction. Tony grabbed the card when it slid out of the slot. He then stormed off toward his car without thanking the man for his help.

Back in his car, by then 5:50, Tony was trying hard to figure out how to deal with yet another setback. His most urgent need was the $1100 to score the weed from Poncho that he needed for Crank. And he had to do everything by eight o'clock. If he didn't make that delivery, he would have a bunch of motorcycle outlaws after him, which would not be an ideal situation.

Then he thought of Fatty. He should have that much.

When Fatty answered Tony's call, he wasn't as friendly as he usually was. "Hey, Tony. What's up, man? You missed the drop today. Put me in a bind. That's not good for business," he said. He was mollified somewhat when Tony told him about the robbery.

"I'm in a bind, too, Fatty. I need a short-term loan. $1100 until tomorrow," Tony said. After hassling back and forth a while, Fatty agreed to the loan, but required next-day repayment of $1500. He then added, "This is gonna tap me out, man. Make sure you make good tomorrow morning. If you don't, we're both gonna have problems."

Tony reluctantly agreed to the outrageous interest and arranged to meet Fatty at the Burgerville on 82nd at 7 p.m. Tony calculated that he could get the $1100 from Fatty, shoot over to his house for the $4500 he had and the $400 from Zack, then meet Poncho by 8. It was gonna be tight. But if nothing went wrong, it should work. He then punched in Poncho's number.

Poncho answered on the first ring. He didn't sound too happy when he said, "Tony. What's up?"

"Hey, amigo. Good news. I got the money. I can meet you at 8 at the usual place."

That's when the roof caved in.

Poncho said, "I can't make it if it's that late. I told you, I got something going on then. I can do it at 7:30. No later. And the price is now $7500. This messing around is screwing up my plans. I don't like that, *amigo*."

"Come on, Poncho. You gotta help me. I'm in a bind. I need the merchandise tonight or I'm in big trouble. I could pay the extra $1500 tomorrow," Tony pleaded.

After a brief pause, Poncho said, "Hey, man. Sounds like you're in a panic situation. Panic means loss of control. Loss of control means danger. And danger means risk. I don't do risk. As of this minute you and me are done. Over! Comprende? Don't call me again. It wouldn't be good for your health if you did."

"Poncho! Wait a minute!" Tony cried before he realized the line was dead.

With no chance of getting the pot from Poncho, in desperation Tony called Fatty again.

It's me, he said when Fatty answered. "Change of plan. I need

two pounds of good stuff. Can you supply it? The price will be right."

Unable to conceal his surprise, Fatty blurted out, "What you talking about, man? I'm the guy who buys from you. Not the other way round. What's going on?"

Tony, not wanting to get into details, said, "I need it for a drop later tonight. I'll pay you tomorrow and throw in a bonus."

"I don't know why you're asking me for this stuff. You should know I never have that much on hand. And even if I did, it wouldn't be high-test buds you need for one of your preferred customers. Don't think I don't know that you pawn off the dregs on me. I can't help you, man. Let me know if you have anything for me next week. I might be able to use it, although when you didn't show today, I had to buy from another source. Not bad stuff, decent price, too," Fatty said before he rang off.

Checking his watch again, Tony saw that it was already 6:30; three and a half hours until he met Crank. As the seriousness of his situation rapidly escalated, so did his panic. He couldn't call Crank since he didn't have a number for him; those guys were *really* off the grid. The only thing left was to go back to his house. Maybe Zack would have an idea how to get out of this mess.

Tony pulled into the driveway at 7:25. Zack was watching a football game on TV, with the volume way too loud.

"What's up, dude?" Zack yelled when Tony came through the front door, a silly grin on his unshaven, stubbled face.

Tony went over to the TV and switched off the volume, then sat down in the chair across from Zack.

"Got a big problem, man," he said, looking straight into Zack's eyes. That's when he realized that Zack was stoned out of his mind;

glazed eyes, stupid grin, a half-full bowl of cheddar cheese chips on the table, Snickers' wrappers strewn all over the floor.

"I was robbed today. Lost all the stuff I scored this morning that I needed it for the hookup with the motorcycle guy tonight. Can't find a replacement. I'm in big trouble if I don't find two pounds of good pot by 10. Got any ideas?"

Zack looked around the room, then at the soundless football game for a moment, then said, "Did you say something about

motorcycles? You gonna get one? That'd be really cool, dude. I'll get one, too. We can do a road trip . . .. You want some ice cream? There's Rocky Road in the fridge."

"Zack!" Tony screamed. "I'm in trouble! I need some pot."

"Pot?" Zack questioned. "I got no pot left. Smoked the last of it couple of hours ago. Good shit, too. Got some meth. Lots. Want some?"

Tony shook his head, got up from the chair and headed for the kitchen. He grabbed a beer, went out the back door and made his way along the barely visible path to his marijuana plot. He sat down on an old kitchen chair next to the little shed. He nursed his Heineken and stared at the soft clouds moving across the dimming sky. Little puff-ball clouds made him think of snowflakes blowing around in a gentle breeze. The peaceful mood eased him into a trance-like sleep. The previous thoughts of snow must have prompted his dream of cocaine, which morphed into visions of its big bad brother, crystal meth. Then suddenly, still half-asleep, the solution popped into his head.

I'll be honest with Crank and tell him about the robbery, he thought as he came fully to his senses. *Then I'll give him an ounce of Zack's meth. Free. The gang can make just as much from that as they would from two pounds of weed. I'll assure him that I'll have the pot for him in two weeks, back on schedule.* It was 8:45. I better get this organized, he mumbled to himself as he started back to the house.

Carrying his backpack like always, Tony entered Billy's Bar and Grill at 10:05. He saw Crank in his usual back corner booth and quickly made his way through the crowd and slid onto a bench across from the big man. A half-full bottle of tequila, a full shot glass and a full bottle of Coors were in front of him. Four empty beer bottles stood near the edge of the splattered tabletop.

"You're late," Crank said, then picked up the shot glass and downed the contents in one gulp. He poured another shot, letting the amber-colored liquid spill over onto the table. He looked at Tony, who as of yet had said nothing, and spat out, "I need four pounds. My other source got busted. Bring two more tomorrow night. And don't be late."

By then, beads of sweat had formed on Tony's forehead. His voice was strained when he got up the nerve to say, "Uh . . . Crank. We got a little problem. I've got the home-grown for you. But some Mexican cartel guys stole my stash of Mexican, the stuff I had for you tonight. It's gonna take me a few weeks to put together what you need. But I'll do it. Don't worry. You can depend on me. And as an expression of my good faith, here's an ounce of highly pure meth. Gratis. Your guys can do okay with this."

Crank listened to Tony in silence. About five seconds after Tony stopped talking, he suddenly raised his log-like arm and smashed it down on the table like a pile driver ramming its target. The empties bounced off the table edge and landed on the concrete floor. Glass shards filled the air. No one in the bar bothered to look their way.

"You telling me you didn't bring any of the good stuff?" Crank said in a low, menacing voice.

"Yeah, but this crystal should make up for it, "Tony said as he slid the baggie across the table.

"Crystal?" Crank said, swiping the baggie off the table with his gigantic tattoo-covered hand. "Our guys produce that much every ten minutes. We don't need your little piss-ant gift. What I *need* is your high-end pot!" his voice rapidly rising in mounting anger. "We got customers we gotta take care of. I was depending on you. Now you've messed me up real bad." The threat of violence was escalating. It radiated from Crank's unfocused eyes. The long scar on his cheek was growing redder by the second.

Suddenly Crank thrust his arm forward and grabbed Tony's shirt in his fist. "We're going outside for a walk," he said.

Tony knew he had to do something fast or in five minutes he would either be beaten to a pulp or dead.

He quickly fished his keys from his jacket pocket, held the long house key tightly, flung his arm out and jabbed it as hard as he could into Crank's right eye.

Crank let go of Tony's shirt and let out an agonizing scream as viscous fluid mixed with blood spurted from what little was left of his eyeball.

Tony shot out of the booth and headed to the door before Crank had a chance to grab him again. Tony glanced back over his shoulder

and saw the big man jump up and look his way, toss the table aside and start running toward him, seemingly ignoring his damaged eye. Maybe it was the booze, or the uncontrolled rage, but as Crank was almost close enough to reach Tony, he smashed into a chair and fell forward onto the floor, swearing and screaming incoherently.

Tony rushed to his car, which was parked next to Crank's Harley, got in and started it. When he glanced at the bar's front door, he saw Crank charging out. Tony backed up a few feet, then sped forward, ramming full force into the rear of the bike. Its tire exploded and the frame was mangled. He tore out of the parking lot, leaving the raging giant engulfed in a thick cloud of gritty dust.

Three months later, on a gorgeous, clear fall morning, Tony and Angie were sitting on her patio sharing a pot of coffee and a platter of her fresh-baked bran muffins. Mt Hood was revealed in all its glory to the east. The flat top of Mt. St. Helens was visible to the north.

"How's your accounting class going? Don't you have an exam sometime this week?" Angie asked.

"No problem. I'm still acing that class," he answered confidently. Tony was enrolled in a business track at Portland Community College and doing well. He really liked it, and even had thoughts of college when he finished at PCC. He was living with Angie and had a part-time job as a barista at Pete's. She had agreed to help him if he severed all connections with the illegal drug world, joined the grid as a legitimate citizen and got an education. He accepted her terms and was actually glad he did. Life was looking up. He felt good about himself and what he was doing. He could even see a future for himself.

His first class that morning was at ten.

"I better get going, Sis. Don't wanna be late."

Tony closed his laptop, gathered his books and stuffed it all into his pack. Heading for the door, he yelled, "See you tonight. Have a nice day."

He went out the front door into a manicured courtyard and down the walkway that led to the street where his car was parked. When he reached the street, he stopped short. Six big Harley Davidson motorcycles were parked in the yellow-striped no-parking zone in

front of the apartment complex. Standing next to them were six scary-looking men clad in black leather. The huge one with the patch over his right eye socket said, "Morning, Tony. How ya doin? It's such a nice day we thought we'd take you and your sister for a ride."

Memory

By Mizeta Moon

When I woke, I had never existed.

I had no remembrance of past events.

Did not know the name of anything my eyes encountered.

I had to be schooled and had to learn.

I was a canvas awaiting color.

"She's awake," someone uttered.

"Guard every word. She absorbs and imprints everything."

I would later learn that I was on a train. Traveling through a country named England, bound for France. Eventually, I would tour the globe, view exotic lands, and experience every clime. Taste food of every nation.

I would sample every essence and touch each culture's cloth.

I would spend a decade living among humans and traveling their world.

I woke to a black-haired, skinny woman who told me she was my aunt. Later, I learned that we were not kin, but tutor and student. A blonde, blue-eyed young woman introduced herself as my maid, but instead, she was there to aid my emotional development. I also had bodyguards who were unobtrusive with their presence. I was told, when my emotions congealed and I could understand such devotion, that they would have gladly sacrificed their lives for me. The process of awakening was a constant revelation, expanding my knowledge exponentially. Those days of traveling filled my data banks with the entire human experience of that time. Made me who

I am in the archive. Gave me a role to fulfill and allowed me to be the next link in endless tomorrows.

During that first trip they taught me that teeth were teeth, eyes were eyes and that hands were multi-purpose tools, utilized by every life form capable of using devices and weapons to establish dominance. They taught me to know beauty as a tangible thing and instilled an appreciation of what Earth had to offer. Why it had to be recorded, reproduced, and preserved.

I saw so much that I cannot tell you in one breath. How wonderful the world is and how beautiful each moment is as it passes. I felt every nuance. I catalogued. I bonded. My design specifications had been measured to the nth degree, therefore I performed as expected. I imprinted, understood, and could act out any human persona of that era.

After ten years of cognizance, my mentors declared that I was ready to return home. I had absorbed enough information to perform my function. Discovering from whence and where I came would be a revelation, leading to fascination as I rejoined the matrix that spawned me.

I left the surface. Was transported to a huge underground complex filled with hallways leading to a myriad of auditoriums. Within each one was a stage. Each of them was set with a specific time frame's furnishings, and upon each stage was an actor dressed in period costume. I learned that we were expected to perform different parts each day, and that the bits would be melded into videos broadcast throughout the galaxy. All of the information I had assimilated about Earth's current state of affairs would soon be sent winging across electronic seas. I felt privileged to be chosen as I began to meet other memory units. They were catalogs filled with centuries of time and thousands of cultures. Some spoke of extinct civilizations, but my decade was barely beginning to bleed its influence into the future. They marveled at my youth and my descriptions of how the world had changed since their time.

We co-mingled during our off time as we are emotional beings as well as data collectors. During those times we explored commonalities, discussed tragedies, laughed and cried in equal measures. I became part of a family. Felt love, though I could not procreate. Was female but possessed no fertile womb. Only the creators could build such a unit as myself.

My next stage of development was truly a process of discovery. I had to learn which of my billions of personalities would rule and serve as the foundation all of my characters could depend upon to be consistent. Portraying the mercurial nature of humanity was challenging, to say the least. Up until that point, I had watched, rather than acted.

As I became more confident at acting out, my videos became popular and were in great demand. Planets I'd never heard of requested more bandwidth. I am constantly on-stage, going from costume to costume, projecting endless roles.

When I first awoke, I was but a child. I grew. I learned. I spoke. But I knew nothing of the world. Now, I clasp my memories to my breast, and cling to them as if they were my ova. My time on the surface was limited, but it was mine alone. I was given the privilege to remember that I once felt open space. That I breathed fresh air. And that I saw the beauty of a rainbow filling a bright blue sky.

On the Way to Brooklyn

By Howard Schneider

On the day before Christmas, Al Badowski and his wife Phyllis, and their two kids, thirteen-year-old Patty and her little brother Jason, were stuck in heavy traffic on Route Nine a little south of Catskill, New York. They were headed to Al's parents' house in Brooklyn, intending to arrive in time for five-o'clock cocktails before their annual Christmas eve dinner.

Crawling along at five miles an hour, Phyllis angrily switched from her book CD to an AM traffic station. She was concerned about the worsening weather—heavy rain was already making the wipers work extra hard just to maintain visibility.

They learned that a heating-oil truck had turned over about twenty miles ahead; traffic would be blocked for the rest of the day. Even worse, none of the detours were near where they were stuck.

"Patty, give me your phone. My battery's dead and I need to do a map-search," Phyllis said over her shoulder.

"Mom, I'm texting. Use Dad's." Patty snapped back.

"Your father forgot his. It's in the pocket of his other coat. Give me yours. I gotta figure out how to get around this disaster."

A few minutes later Phyllis said, "Take the next right—Malta Avenue. We can bypass the wreck and get back on Route Nine in about thirty miles.

"Where will it take us," Al asked.

"Along the east side of a big reservoir. Just leave it to your navigator. I'll take care of it," Phyllis answered, trying to lift the mood a bit.

"Mom! Jenny's waiting."

"Okay, okay," Phyllis said, passing the phone back to her daughter.

As soon as Al turned onto Malta, Patty said, "Mom, what'd you do to the phone? The battery's dead. I need the charger."

"It was already low. You should have charged it before we left home," Phyllis said, rifling through the glove compartment.

"What am I supposed to do now? I need to use it!"

Paying no attention to her angry daughter, Phyllis said, "Al . . . where's the damn charger?"

"Uh… uh, I think it might be in the other car."

"How many times have I told you to buy another one of these things so this won't keep happening?" Phyllis said.

"Sorry, babe. We were so rushed getting out of the house I forgot about it.

"Daaad. How can you be such a screw-up? Now I can't text Jenny. She's gonna think we had a wreck or something."

Al ignored his distraught daughter and concentrated on driving. The rain had turned to sleet and was making a worse mess on the window, and ice was beginning to build up on the road. He felt the slickness increase as they got closer to the big body of water, and heavy clouds were darkening an already shortened winter afternoon. The reduced visibility made it difficult for him to stay in his lane.

Finally, they reached the reservoir and turned south along the shore. Ten minutes later the twisting road started a slight climb, and when they rounded a sharp curve they suddenly encountered blinking red lights. Al hit the brakes and came to a sliding halt next to a state trooper parked across the road. He lowered his window when the trooper approached.

"Better slow down, sir. Ice is building up real fast. The road's closed up ahead. A landslide blocked both lanes. You'll have to go back the way you came."

"Is there any way around it? We've got to be in New York City soon. And Route Nine's closed."

"There's a county road over that hill," the trooper said, pointing west. "It rejoins this road on the other side of the landslide. But there may be some snow up there. Ice, too. I wouldn't recommend it without four-wheel drive or snow-tires.

"This Chrysler holds the road real good. We won't have any problems. Where's the turn-off?"

"Back about half a mile. Just after a big red house. You gonna try it?"

"Yeah. We've already lost too much time." Al made a U-turn and headed north, easily finding the road the officer described. It was a narrow blacktop that meandered through a densely wooded range of hills and quickly increased in elevation. The snowfall became heavier as they climbed; thick wet slush accumulated on the front window except where the wipers were barely able to clear it away.

They'd been on that road about twenty minutes when Jason, who until then had been focused on his Game Boy, said, "Mom, I gotta to go to the bathroom."

"You have to hold it till we get to a gas station or a McDonald's."

"I can't. I gotta go now. Can't we stop for a minute?"

"There's no place to pull over," Al interjected defiantly.

Then Phyllis said, "Albert! No other cars are gonna come along here. We're in the middle of god-forsaken nowhere. Stop and let him out. It'll only take a minute."

"All right, but I don't like it," Al replied. "Just make it fast. We gotta get out of this mess." He took his foot off the gas and gently applied the brakes. But even as gently as he did, the big car started sliding on a patch of ice, shifting to the right because of to the road's slope away from the center. No matter what he did, Al couldn't keep to a straight line; the momentum was too great and the surface too slick. Then, totally out of control, the car slid off the side, crashed half-way into a rocky snow-covered ditch, and came to a jarring halt. It was at a thirty-degree angle with the left-side tires suspended in mid-air spinning wildly and the underside caught on the raised berm.

Phyllis and Patty screamed. Al swore and pounded violently on the steering wheel. Jason burst into tears.

"Oh, my God!" Phyllis then shouted. "What are we gonna do?"

"Are we gonna die?" Patty cried.

"Daddy. I gotta pee!" Jason pleaded between sobs.

"Calm down!" Al yelled. "Phyllis, shut up. Jason! Open the door and do your business. Patty, check your phone again."

A second later she said, "It's still dead, Dad."

Phyllis started to blurt out something but abruptly caught herself, reining in her rage. Then she calmly said, "Al—we can't sit here until the gas runs out. We'll freeze to death. Unless a car comes along soon, you'll have to go for help."

"Are you crazy? It's too far. And it's too cold."

"Al! You have to! You can walk back to the main road. It can't be more than five miles."

"I'm not dressed for a hike like that. I'd never make it."

"Get your snow boots and parka out of the trunk. We'll be okay with the engine and heater running if you start now."

"Uh . . . I left the boots and parka at home. There wasn't room after I got all the food and presents and damn luggage in."

"What? Well, you can't walk five miles in a foot of snow in those stupid loafers and that thin jacket. Oh, my God. We *are* in trouble, aren't we?"

Just then Jason climbed back into the car, shivering from the cold.

And Patty sat whimpering like an abandoned baby, the dead phone clutched in her clinched fist. "Mom. We're gonna die, aren't we."

But then, without warning, there was a soft tap on the driver-side window.

"Thank God," Phyllis said, looking past Al to see who it was.

Al lowered the window to reveal a scraggly-bearded old man peering at him. "Are we ever glad to see you! We're in a bit of trouble. Do you have a phone we can use?"

"No. Never needed one. Looks like you're halfway into that ditch," the old man said. "Probably hung up on the undercarriage. You need a tow."

"Yes, sir. We sure do. Do you have a four-wheel-drive vehicle, and a tow chain or strong rope?"

"No, nothing like that. But my friend might be able to help. He could probably pull you free."

"Can he get here soon? Does he have a tow truck or something?"

"He's on a break right now, but I'll call him anyway." The old man stepped away from the car, looked into the woods bordering the road and whistled a single long note.

A minute later there was a sound of something crashing through brush and low-hanging tree limbs. Then a huge form appeared at the edge of the dark woods. Its glimmering eyes were focused on the old man.

In the darkness, Al and the others couldn't tell what it was. Then, apparently in response to some subtle signal, it started coming closer, its shape gradually becoming apparent. It was a gigantic deer, or perhaps an elk. It had a huge antlers and a thick neck and broad chest, and it projected incredible strength. When it reached the old man, it stopped and remained perfectly still, as if awaiting instructions.

Leaving the stately beast where it stood, the old man walked up the road a way, then returned a minute later holding a heavy harness which he slipped onto the patiently waiting animal. He mumbled a few words that Al couldn't hear, then came back to the car window. "When I signal, hang on tight." A few seconds later he waved at Al, then said something to animal. The the huge creature lunged forward, and the car sprang into the air with a jarring jerk and landed squarely on the road with an ear-piercing crash. A churning trail of snow, ice, and gravel swirled behind. The whole family cheered, and Phyllis and Patty wiped away tears of relief.

Al climbed out of the car, ignored the wet cold penetrating his flimsy shoes, and ran to where the old man was undoing the harness. His wallet was in one hand and several bills in the other. "Here, sir. This for your trouble. You saved our lives."

The old man glanced at the bills and said, "Keep your money, Al. Your thanks are sufficient."

Al wondered how the old man knew his name, but instead of asking about that, said, "What kind of animal *is* that? It bigger than a deer, and those antlers are enormous."

"A Siberian reindeer. Goes by the name Rudolph. Maybe you've heard of him. Anyway, we have to be on our way. Still lots of work to do."

With that said, the old man turned toward the woods and whistled two loud blasts. Before Al was back in the driver's seat and ready to drive off, eight more reindeer had emerged from the forest and made their way to the sled and formed two columns. Soon the old man had them harnessed. Rudolph was in the lead. In no time the old man was in the sled and tearing past the car. As he sped by, he cried out—

"Merry Christmas to all, and to all a good night."

Wednesday Night in Tijuana

By Mizeta Moon

Marge was still talking when Burton rolled his big Caddy up to the border crossing barricade. She'd yakked non-stop from Topeka. His mind had become a failing defense screen and during the last few hours he'd stared at the road without really seeing it.

"Are you sure you got the Mexican car insurance?"

For the forty fifth time.

"Make sure I get to pee before we get too far from civilized plumbing."

For the hundredth time . . . Like the story of her ex-husband that grew more imaginative each time it was told. Burton hated Marge's ex-husband for passing her off to him when the load became too heavy. He hated himself for being a lonely fool who thought he needed her at the time.

This Mexican vacation had been her idea, of course. All the ideas were hers. For once, Burton didn't mind playing along. If all went well, he might find a senorita who'd get naked for a price. This fantasy kept him sane during long hours on the faceless freeway system. Now that they'd arrived, he would have to keep his emotions in check. If Marge became suspicious, she might not take her afternoon nap that gave him his play time.

Tijuana was a boiling cauldron of energy. Definitely not white bread and low-cal margarine. Earthy, raw, bustling, and blaring. After they'd parked the car and checked into their room, Marge wanted to see it all. Himself, he could have used a few z's and a slug of tequila. Due to his tiredness, the city was assailing his senses and overloading him.

"At least let me take a shower for Christ's sake."

He stood beneath the hot cascade for as long as she would allow. When she got loud with her demand for urgency, he toweled off and dressed. Resigned, he led her down the stairway to the street and embarked on an odyssey into the bizarre.

Section four liberty commences in five minutes. Five minutes to section four liberty. Civilian clothing authorized. Liberty card required for boarding. All hands muster 0800 hours.

Most of the trouble they got into was due to Kowalky. He had a nose for situations best left alone. One shore leave he beat up a pimp for abusing a hooker, who then stabbed him by way of thanks. It was always something, but for some reason they kept taking him along. Maybe they secretly craved excitement. Maybe they were masochists. Martin wasn't sure and deep down really didn't care. It was only when they were in jail or bleeding in the street that he wanted to strangle Kowalky.

Hogan was the best at ignoring Kowalky's antics. He'd order pitchers and drink beer till dawn, then go stand muster and sleep for the rest of the day. Hogan's job required little attention when they were in port. Anyway, tonight they were going to Tijuana. Martin had never made port in San Diego. He'd heard lots of stories about the tourist mecca that lie only a few miles from their berth. He tingled with excitement as they walked off the gangplank, hopped into a cab and said.

"Tijuana, my man."

Like a bunch of high school kids, they punched each other and laughed while debating who would do what and who wouldn't. The cabbie got pissed off, so they settled for nervous giggling and pretended to behave.

They walked across the border and got their first taste of a different world. Vendors hawking goods; pleading, whining or bullying to make a sale. Desperate eyes and voices willing to barter about the price of anything. Silver necklaces twined around a lean brown arm. A group of Indian women with bare dirty feet, cracked and dry from poverty and abuse; selling gum and beads laid on a sidewalk blanket. To Martin it looked like utter chaos. Even the smells were foreign and overwhelming in their intensity. They'd barely started down Revolucion Avenue when Kowalky wanted to find a tittie bar and down a few beers. For once they were all of a like mind and crowded into a joint whose music blared into the street. The doorman ushered them in with the suave coolness of a shepherd leading lambs to slaughter. When spenders arrived, girls half asleep in booths along an outer wall transformed into tigresses on the prowl for pesos.

Martin cringed at the four-dollar-price for a margarita. Hogan shrugged, paid for a pitcher of beer, then drank directly from it. On stage, an over-the-hill stripper was grinding out a frenetic version of Wooly Bully. Kowalky was already looking around with that eye that always found trouble. Martin felt like slapping him, but the man was too far away. Instead, he turned to their other buddy, Farrell, who'd also been cut by the hooker.

"I don't want any crap tonight. And I'm not making this my final destination. I want to see more of Mexico than the inside of a rundown tittie bar."

"Okay, man. Chill for a while and we'll split."

Martin let himself be pacified for the moment. Hogan started on another pitcher and the music switched to Michael Jackson's Thriller. At least the next dancer had a good body, even if he didn't like her face.

Marge loved tacos and served them regularly to the ladies' auxiliary back home. The little dears would wolf them down, then complain about how the spices affected their delicate constitutions. Alone at home with Burton, she would heap her plate, then plow through them wholesale while guzzling a quart of beer straight from the bottle.

Although Burton was drawn to the tantalizing odors coming from sidewalk stands, he refused to eat outside their hotel. Hot roasting peppers, sizzling meats and tortillas were tempting, but he remained staunch. He'd heard too many tales of Montezuma's revenge to take the matter of food poisoning lightly.

A roving band of mariachis coaxed them out of five bucks for a couple songs. Marge smiled and swayed to the music and gave Burton the look that said she was feeling romantic, but when the band stopped playing the next taco stand caught her attention. She dragged Burton through the teeming crowd towards a string of glaring naked lightbulbs and a column of smoke.

Hands. A veritable sea of hands. Coaxing. Cajoling. Gently steering the elbow towards rack after rack of merchandise.

"I'll make you the best deal in the history of business. Come into my shop, senor."

Hypnotically trying to unleash the tourists' spending urges and send them back across the border laden with souvenirs. Burton didn't want anything but a woman. He kept alert for places he could explore during the free time he hoped to have. Some of the women he saw were so beautiful he wanted to stop and stare. Instead, he forced himself to nod every so often so Marge would think he was paying rapt attention to the multi-colored serapes thrust in front of them, or, a minute later, by the fiftieth rendition of her surgery.

After a dozen taco stands and nearly as many beers, Marge was looking hammered. Her eyes were glassy, and she began to weave. Burton wanted to hail a taxi, but Marge insisted on walking back to the hotel. He was trudging deeper into the maze, but never saw its walls closing in.

Reno and Renee would have avoided the scene about to play out had she not gotten a rock in her shoe. The two lovers had been walking through Tijuana's familiar streets for hours. Hand in hand they traveled inside their personal bubble as their wanderings brought back memories of when they'd first met.

He still remembered the first time he'd seen her red hair and creamy skin. She'd just ordered a Corona at the Hard Rock Café and smiled at him pleasantly. He'd stood dumbstruck while gathering the courage to approach her.

She remembered his lost puppy-dog-look. The timing was right, as she'd just freed herself from a cumbersome relationship. The crowded club, slow service, and a few beers gave him enough time to capture her attention.

Neither expected it, but their relationship blossomed quickly. Now they were in Tijuana celebrating a year of whirlwind romance. Since they were both San Diegans, the scene in Tijuana was not the least bit confusing. They understood the day-to-day working parts of the city and how they meshed with law and order that casual visitors think doesn't exist.

They'd been about to board one of the old creaking busses that had hauled millions of people over their lifetime when Renee bent down to remove the rock from her shoe. The driver cursed them and drove off, leaving them no choice but to continue on foot. This simple act of rudeness by the driver put them on course to be part of what was about to happen. Had they been clairvoyant, they could have seen it coming. But they weren't, and therefore, didn't realize what was happening till they were knee deep and sinking.

The four tipsy young sailors were walking towards the Jai Alai fronton. Kowalky was trying to talk a hooker into doing all of them for fifty bucks. Martin wanted to go dancing and was lobbying for a night club. Hogan couldn't be convinced that the fronton wasn't open on Wednesdays, so they were going to show him the darkened parking lot. Farrell was hungry and didn't want to eat at a curbside stand. The rest of them didn't want to spend money for food. They could eat for free when they got back to the ship.

Bickering constantly, they strode along at a fast clip, forcing the hooker to struggle to keep pace in her floppy high heels.

"If you want me you better slow down. I won't chase you stupid sailors all night."

For once it wasn't Kowalky that initiated the chain of events. It was Hogan. Kowalky only made it worse when the shouting started. Hogan had decided to offer the hooker twenty bucks to just do him standing up in an alley.

"Police come maybe."

"I'll give you thirty."

She nodded reluctantly and stepped into the dark recesses of the alley. Hogan followed her in, fumbling with his zipper. The rest of them stood at the alley mouth shifting back and forth on suddenly awkward feet. They could hear the sounds as Hogan quenched the fire of his lust. All of them were embarrassed and not amused.

Reno and Renee were about to pass the same alley on the other end of the block. Stumbling towards them were Burton and Marge. They nearly escaped fate's snare, but at the last moment Marge lurched headlong into Reno's chest and they both went sprawling. The result was pure slapstick. Renee and Burton bumped heads while trying to pull Reno out from under Marge. Marge started screaming and thrashing around, which kept Reno pinned. Burton finally managed to get Marge to her feet and Renee began brushing Reno off with her hand. By the time they noticed Marge's purse lying on the sidewalk it was too late. A ten-year-old thief darted between them, grabbed the purse and took off down the alley.

Kowalky was going to be next on the hooker who was being held against the wall by Hogan. He whipped out his penis to take a leak so he could stay hard and ready. When the little thief ran into him it knocked his pants down around his ankles. Thinking he was about to be robbed, Kowalky grabbed the kid and they went down in a heap of thrashing limbs. Meanwhile, the other foursome came running after the thief.

When Marge saw Kowalky grappling with the purse snatcher she only saw his penis waving in the wind. She began beating on him, which allowed the thief to start running again. Reno tripped the boy, and when he fell, Renee jumped onto his back and held him down. The thief was screaming. Kowalky was howling. Marge was cursing everything and everybody. Oblivious to it all, Hogan was trying to finish up with the hooker.

When Burton saw Hogan and the hooker, he couldn't take any more and wrested the now confused and frightened woman away from Hogan. Shoving her back against the wall he rapidly unzipped.

Mine now. Go to sleep Marge. Mine now. Go to sleep.

The hooker kicked Burton in the groin and tried to run away, but her panty hose were still down, and she fell flat on her face. It was then that the flashing lights converged on them from both ends of the alley.

Later, Martin wasn't sure if the sirens, the crowd that watched, or the arrest itself was more embarrassing. All he knew was that once again his service record would get more black marks and his wallet would be emptied by bailing out of the Tijuana jail. The worst part was that he hadn't really done a thing.

The police found a bunch of half-naked drunken gringos brawling in an alley. Amid the babble of voices trying to explain what had happened, they were sympathetic, but in the end, they took everyone to jail except the boy, who they considered an innocent bystander. The Hooker was furious. Marge was mad at

Burton more than the thief. Reno and Renee were indignant because they were

only trying to help.

One by one, they were marched in front of a judge, convicted, and given fines for drunk and disorderly, plus indecent exposure for Kowalky, Hogan, and the hooker. While Marge faced the judge, Burton slipped the hooker their room number and made arrangements for the next day.

Kowalky spit on the floor as they left the jail. The other three vowed that from then on, he was persona-non-grata. Farrell was still moaning about being hungry and Hogan wanted another pitcher of beer. Martin wanted a cab and the solace of his narrow bunk.

Reno and Renee were the last to get released. Upon leaving the building, they saw Burton following Marge down the street, begging forgiveness. Marge looked like the prow of a ship steaming through the crowds. When she stopped at a taco stand Burton felt everything had returned to normal.

One Incredible Evening

By Mizeta Moon

Suffice to say that we were all amazed. When the one-legged man with a monkey on his shoulder hobbled in on a crutch, most of us looked away in disgust, or wondered why such a wretch could be granted admittance. It was the night of the Grand Cotillion and everyone wore their most spectacular wardrobe. Only the highest of high society had been given golden passes. All in attendance were dismayed, but soon this man and his beast would evoke sorrow, joy and wonder in our hearts and minds when they shared the music of their souls. We would be captivated. Enmeshed in a moment unraveling in time.

Quite a stir arose at first. Captains of industry took exception. Ladies prone to do so, became faint. The mere presence of such a diseased fellow and his companion was an affront our host would be sorely tested to explain.

The monkey leapt down from the man's shoulder almost immediately. It scurried to a table laden with succulent fruits and began eating greedily. Its keeper thumped across the parquet dance floor on his weather-beaten, hand-hewn support and urged the monkey to return to his perch.

We were appalled. No person of good standing could eat from that table again. When the monkey pawed its way back onto the man, one could hear a collective sigh of relief.

As the sergeant-at-arms stood poised to lay hands on the intruder and oust him, our host bade everyone be silent. All eyes were drawn to him as he spoke.

You thirst for the unusual, and I also feel such yearning. When

I look into your hearts, I know that you want more. You crave
something outside what you've experienced to this moment. It is a
gnawing in the belly that spirals you towards despondency when it
remains beyond your grasp. The mind seeks, but no fulfillment is
granted. I understand that need and seek to provide relief from
your anguish.

Bowing to the gathering as if he were a thespian, our host
continued. I bring to you tonight that experience you desire.
Something so beyond imagination that some might accuse me of
witchcraft. So be it—let me be hanged should I be judged of such
malfeasance. Ladies, honored guests, and fine gentlemen, without
further ado, I present a spectacle for the ages.

As we sat stunned, not knowing how to respond, the one-
legged man broke open his coat-front and revealed a violin. He
passed the instrument to the monkey, who accepted the instrument
and then jumped to the floor. From his pocket, the man produced a
set of finger cymbals and began playing them softly in a
compelling cadence.

The monkey reached under his hat and produced a block of
resin, which he began to rub across his lengthy tail. Seconds later,
with what appeared to be a nod of satisfaction, the monkey
wrapped spiny fingers around his tail, bowed the strings as only a
maestro could, and transported us to a state of astonishment.

He played like a beast run amok. It was a concerto of primal
joy that unleashed our own bestial urges. After being taken on a
journey of musical delight that soared and plummeted through an
incredible range of feelings, there was naught else to be said. That
monkey touched us in the deepest recesses of our souls, and we
shall never be the same.

I often wonder what happened to them. Do they wander dark
streets at night?

Do they hunger? Thirst? Find audience? Sleep in safety?

That night remains firmly lodged in my mind. A beautiful
room full of privileged people, dancing and swaying to the tunes of
a mad monkey. With its feet set firmly on the ground and its
companion keeping beat, they ascended to remarkable heights and
took everyone present with them.

Like Mama

By Howard Schneider

The big woman's anger exploded in a loud outburst. "Girl! You ain't nothing but a dumb crack baby. Just cuz you five years old don't mean you any smarter than when you was born. Seems all I do is clean up after you. Git outta here. I don't want to see your face one more time today. You hear?"

Celia scrambled to slide off her chair where spilt milk ran over the edge of the table onto a filthy linoleum floor. She scurried out the kitchen door, ducking under the slap Mrs. Hammond aimed at her. She ran as fast as she could down a dimly lit hall to the little room she shared with two other foster kids, grabbed her only doll off her cot, and went into a dank closet. Sitting in the dark, rocking the thrift-shop ragdoll in her arms, she began singing a soft lullaby, making up words and melody as she went.

It was a year later when Candice Kane, a dedicated county child-care social worker, rescued the foster children from the Hammonds and found new homes for them. Celia wound up with the Bensons, an African American couple whose six-year old daughter died of leukemia two years earlier.

"We'll take good care of this pretty little girl. Don't you worry one single minute about that," Mrs. Benson said, crouching down and enfolding little Celia in her ample arms.

Her first day of kindergarten was a disaster. Celia's lack of social skills and below average intelligence were obvious to the teacher and explained why the little girl was at such a loss. She sat alone in a corner, trembling with fear and confusion. The next day Celia was placed in a special needs class with other kids like her and an understanding and dedicated teacher. When Miss Kane visited the following week, she was optimistic that everything would be okay. Her job was to make sure it was.

Twelve years passed quickly. Patient tutoring by Mr. Benson (who was a high school history teacher), along with Mrs. Benson getting Celia into her church's youth choir, and Miss Kane's hawk-like attention, ensured that Celia did the best she could under the circumstances. In spite of the use of crack cocaine by her mother while pregnant, and cruel neglect during the year before Celia was thrown into the foster care system, Celia gradually blossomed into an impressive young woman.

A life-changing event for Celia occurred when she tried out for the high school freshman choir. She was nervous and scared when the director called her in for an audition from where she had been waiting in the hall with a dozen other kids. Mr. Clemson greeted her without looking up from the form describing each candidate, seemingly anxious to get through the auditions as fast as possible.

"Miss Bloom, would you please sing the song from that sheet music on the stand?"

"I'm sorry, sir, but I don't read music. Can I just sing something I know?"

His frown was a mixture of irritation and curiosity.

"It says here that you're in a church choir. How can that be if you can't read the notes?"

"After I hear it once I can sing it."

"That may be acceptable for some, but not in my choir. When you learn to sight-read, come back for an audition. On your way out ask Helen Smithers to come in."

Celia was devastated by the choir director's cursory dismissal. Music was a mainstay of her life. The one passion that brought not only joy, but also a feeling of self-worth, a feeling that there was at least one thing she could do as well as others could.

When Miss Kane learned about Celia's rejection, she took matters into her own hands and called her friend, Lenny Brown. Lenny was the director of the city-wide gospel choir and always on the lookout for talent. He'd made it big in the Chicago jazz and blues scene forty years earlier, and now, even as he approached seventy, was a sought-after keyboard player and teacher. His work with the gospel choir was a labor of love, which was his payback for all the good fortune that had come his way.

Brown looked up when Celia walked through the door to the basement music room the gospel choir rented. He waved her over to where he sat at a piano playing chord progressions. The puzzled look on her face caught his attention.

"Jazz," he said. "You like the sound?"

"I'm not sure. It's different from anything I've heard before. I mostly sing church music. I like gospel most of all."

"Then you're in the right place. Miss Kane said you don't read music, but that you have a good voice—and a good ear, as well. But before we get to the singing, I'd like to know a little about you," he said in a friendly manner. "Take off your coat and have a seat." He stood up, then pulled a nearby chair closer. "We don't have to be in a hurry."

Sitting next to the piano, Celia began. "I'm a foster kid and live with Mr. and Mrs. Benson. I like it there. They're not like the ones I was with before . . . I'm 18 and a freshman at Central High. I'm older than the other freshmen because I had to repeat third and fifth grades . . . They say I'm a slow learner because something's wrong with my brain. . . . Mr. Benson helps me with homework, so I keep up okay. . . . I like to sing. It makes me feel good. . . . They say my mama was a singer. Maybe that's why I like it so much. She died when I was little. I don't remember her. . . . Miss Kane told me to see you about your choir. The director didn't let me into the one at school."

Lenny stared intently at the girl for a long moment, then, breaking the awkward silence, said, "Uh . . . how do you manage in your church choir if you can't read music?"

"I listen to the song, then I can sing it, "she replied. "I like to do the harmony, too."

"You *must* have a good ear. You memorize the words, as well?"

"Yes, sir. My memory for music is better than for other things."

"Well, in that case, why don't you sing one of the gospel hymns you do at church."

"We're working on 'Down by the Riverside' for next Sunday.

Would that be okay?"

"Yeah, sure. It's a great old spiritual. Mahalia Jackson recorded it way back in the day. Whenever you're ready."

As soon as Celia sang the first line, "Gonna lay down my burdens, down by the riverside," Lenny knew he was witnessing something rare. As she continued, he was astonished by what he was hearing: the sound, the purity, the power, as if she were channeling Mahalia herself, maybe just a little bit sweeter, but still strong, thrilling, and uplifting at the same time. But there was something else, too. Just as he had felt a remote familiarity when he first laid eyes on her, he had a similar feeling about her voice.

Then it came to him.

"My God," he exclaimed after Celia sang the last note.

"Was that okay?" she asked before he was able to say anything else.

"Yes, it sure was," he said emphatically. "In fact, it was a lot more than just okay. It was amazing. You have a wonderful talent. A gift. I'd be happy to have you in the choir. I'll teach you how to read music too."

Her face lit up. "Thank you, Mr. Brown. I was hoping you would accept me. I was worried about not being able to read notes."

"You don't have to be concerned about that. But . . . there is something else I want to ask you. What do you know about your mother? What was her name?"

"On my birth certificate it's Florence Washington. My last name is Bloom, like my father."

When Celia revealed her mother's name, Lenny was temporarily speechless, overcome with emotion and memories.

After he recovered, he said, "I knew your mother. I was the one who discovered her. It was in 1985. I heard her do a solo in the Greater Salem Baptist Church."

"You knew my mother?" Celia asked, her voice wavering.

"Yes. She was a remarkable singer. A natural. I introduced her to the Chicago blues scene and arranged her first gigs. In no time she was making a name for herself, singing with the best of the local bands."

"What was she like? I don't know anything about her."

"She was a wonderful woman—smart, talented, and hard-working. Sadly, she fell in with a bad crowd and got into drugs. Her career took a nosedive. Nothing I nor any of her other friends could do about it. She wasn't able to overcome her addiction to crack cocaine."

"Nobody told me about her before. Was she a good person?"

"Yes, the best. A mother you can be proud of."

"I still miss her," he added after a moment, unable to disguise the sadness in his voice.

"I never knew anything about her, but I miss her too," Celia said.

"I remember when you were born. I lost track of you when the agency took you away. You must have been about a year old. By then your father, Harry Bloom, was long gone. Florence died a month or so later."

After a long silence, Celia spoke. She was on the verge of crying; tears were welling up in her eyes. "Thank you for telling me about her. Knowing who she was makes me want to take up where she left off. Do you think I could?"

"Yes. I do. I think you have what it takes," he replied.

"Will you help me?" she asked softly.

"Yes, Celia. I will. It would be an honor. . . and a privilege, "he replied as he wiped away his own tears.

Acknowledgements

We want to thank Jill Powell and Raina Glazener for their insightful editorial comments. Thanks also to Nancy Woods, founder and leader of the Kickstart writing program in Portland, who provided editorial comments for Monkeys in the Mango Trees. Special thanks goes to the Hollywood Senior Center (Portland, Oregon) for hosting the Writers Unite group that allowed the authors to meet and collaborate on this collection of stories. If you've enjoyed our book, we would love to have you donate money, time, clothing or food to a senior center near you. Such facilities serve many who need help, company, friends, or often just someplace to go.

Howard Schneider
Mizeta Moon
Linda Burk